A CHILLING CHRISTMAS EVE

A PSYCHOLOGICAL THRILLER

SUSAN SPECHT ORAM

SOS COMMUNICATIONS LLC

A CHILLING CHRISTMAS EVE

A Psychological Thriller

Susan Specht Oram

SOS Communications LLC

Published by SOS Communications LLC in 2025

www.susanspechtoram.com

First Edition

ISBN: 979-8-9937061-2-2 (e-book)

ISBN: 979-8-9937061-3-9 (paperback)

 Formatted with Vellum

1

FRANCESCA

We gathered around the Christmas tree, sipping hot spiced cider, but froze when my phone rang. My eyes flicked around the room, because the two people I cared about most were here with me. I'd told friends not to call, because I'd be busy hosting family on Christmas Eve. My younger brother Troy arched his eyebrows, issuing a silent scolding for leaving my phone on.

Mom said, "I thought we agreed to turn off our phones and celebrate the holiday together."

Troy nodded, scratching his stubbled chin.

My phone rang again. Whoever it was really wanted to reach me on a dark, dreary Christmas eve in the rainy Pacific Northwest. I held my breath and waited for it to stop.

My fingers twitched, and I leaned over, drawn to the

device resting on the coffee table, trying to covertly see who was calling. Despite feeling rude to my brother and mother, I stared at the screen. It must be important for someone to call several times in a row on a night when many people were home with family.

My pulse picked up when I saw the caller's name, and a wave of guilt washed over me. I told Mom, "It's Grandma. I'll answer it."

Mom and Troy frowned. I picked up the phone and said, "Hi, Grandma. Merry Christmas."

"Hello, Francesca, and it's not merry here. I'll tell you why in a minute. Is anyone there with you?"

I bit my lower lip and looked at Mom and my brother. They shook their heads, as if to say I shouldn't tell my grandmother they were here. But it was too late for that, because I wasn't going to keep secrets from my paternal grandmother.

"Mom and Troy are here. We're hanging out, sipping hot cider by the Christmas tree I set up in my new place. If you lived nearby, we'd have you over to celebrate with us."

Cheerful Christmas tunes played in my living room, prancing through a heavy silence over the phone line. I reached over and turned down the volume for the holiday music.

Grandma said, "Put me on speaker phone, and I'll tell all three of you at the same time."

Troy picked at an imaginary piece of lint on my thrift store sofa. I stabbed an index finger at the phone, put it in speaker mode and said, "Okay, Grandma, we're listening."

Troy said, "Merry Christmas, Grandma."

Mom nodded. "Yes, happy holidays. How are you? How's the weather where you are?"

"The weather's just fine in California, but I have bad news, so let's get it over with. Troy and Francesca, your father died."

I clapped a hand to my mouth. Troy gasped. Tears trickled down Mom's cheeks.

My throat tightened with tears. "What do you mean, he died? I thought he was healthy."

"He had a sudden heart attack in his apartment. That was it."

Mom leaned in. "I'm sorry to hear that. When did this happen?"

"Early this afternoon."

The three of us looked at each other. Mom's eyes opened wide and she said in a careful voice she used for my dad's elderly mother, "But that was hours ago. What have you been doing in the meantime?"

Grandma used her most acerbic tone of voice, the one that pushed us away and kept us at a distance, "I've been taking care of things. But you wouldn't know about that because you weren't here, and you never visit."

I wiped tears from my eyes, grieving for the father who left when we were young. He didn't call or write or email much, but when he called, he always said, "When I die, you and Troy will each inherit an apartment building. You'll be millionaires and set for life."

Guilt for not keeping in touch with him, despite his leaving us in the lurch, stabbed at my heart. I cleared my throat. "That's so sad. I'm sorry to hear that. We'll fly down to help you get through this difficult time."

"No, I'm fine. Zane, my gardener, is by my side, and he has been the whole time, helping me."

Troy's mouth fell open. "Your gardener is there? Shouldn't family be helping you instead?"

Grandma sniffed, like she did when she was miffed. "You two children never bothered to call or write your father, or to keep in touch with me all this time. Zane lives in the cottage on my property. He's my right-hand man and the person I trust most."

My brother and I locked eyes, and Mom stared at the Christmas tree decorated with white twinkling lights that seemed inappropriate for a day of sudden sadness and dark grief.

Glancing around the apartment I'd recently moved into, I pursed my lips at the worn tan carpet, a second-hand couch and a chair with a missing arm. I took a plunge into an abyss of clarifying what we've known to be true for years.

"Grandma, we'll fly down and help you sort through his things. And we can talk about the apartment buildings Troy and I inherited and how that'll work, now that Dad is gone."

In a harsh voice, she said, "You greedy children, money is all you think about. You can come visit, but you won't stay with me. You never called or wrote me. You didn't reach out. You were absorbed in your own selfish lives."

Mom spoke up. "Alicia, in their defense, their father said not to bother you because you were busy taking care of his sick dad. And it's a two-way street. You could have written or called, but you didn't. We elders need to set a good example, don't you agree?"

"I did the best I could, given what I was dealing with. They should've called on my birthday, at the very least, or sent cards. They forgot about me."

Words evaporated from my parched mouth, and we sat in silence for a beat.

Grandma said, "That's why I'm leaving my apartment buildings to Zane. He deserves it. He's kind and attentive to me. Isn't that right, Zane?"

A man said, "That's right. Someone has to look after you, and I'm happy to do it."

Mom, Troy and I gazed at each other and held up our hands. This was the first I'd heard about the gardener. I scowled as suspicions flared. I was sure Zane, the supposed gardener, had befriended Grandma to get her money.

The pull to Mill Valley, where Grandma lived north of the Golden Gate Bridge, was strong, and I came up with a plan. Tomorrow, my brother and I would fly south from

Washington State, eliminate Zane from the cozy picture with Grandma and reclaim what was to have been ours.

But first, we needed to finish the conversation and start winning her over to our side. She was haughty, proud and rigid, so it'd take a miracle on Christmas to change her mind.

2

———

FRANCESCA

My pulse picked up when Grandma said we wouldn't get the apartment buildings. Mom put a hand on her stomach, and Troy's mouth fell open. When I was eighteen, Dad told me about the money that would come to me, and I dropped plans to pursue college and a career. I'd be rich when Dad passed away, so why work, I'd reasoned.

Now, I clenched my jaw and told myself to calm down. We had to find a way to change her mind. "Grandma, we'll come be with you. We'll book flights and leave as soon as we can. We'll take over from Zane and support you. You'll be surrounded by family."

Her frosty tone of voice chilled me. "Francesca, call me grandmother. That's what I prefer, but you kids didn't listen. It's a term of respect, and at my age, I deserve that."

I rolled my eyes. She managed to make Dad's death all about her, twisting things around. No wonder he groused about her when I was young and said he didn't like her controlling ways, but he sure grinned when her Christmas and birthday checks for him arrived. One year she sent him a new blue hardtop convertible sports coupe. Although he complained bitterly about her, he left us and moved home to live in one of her apartment buildings. He never did get a job.

I said, "Grandmother, you turned ninety-one last March, isn't that right?"

"You'd know the answer to that, if you kept in touch."

Mom said, "Let's go back to the subject of the apartment buildings the kids were promised. Biff said he wrote it in his will that he was leaving the two buildings to Troy and Francesca."

"That's not true."

Mom said, "That's what he told me, when we last spoke."

Troy and I nodded, and Troy said, "That's what Dad said."

I chimed in. "He did."

"Well, he lied to you. He never drew up a will. He was too lazy to do that."

Mom, Troy and I stared at each other. My stomach knotted, and I cocked my head, thoroughly flummoxed and trying to make sense out of insanity. We deserved the money. He promised us many times, saying we'd each inherit an apartment building. I never expected Dad to shaft us from the grave, but he did.

3

FRANCESCA

I took a sip of spiced cider, but it tasted cold and bitter, so I set the mug down. Dad ruined another holiday, this time with a permanent exit from the planet. When he left us to move to California, it was on a different Christmas Eve. We sat at the table staring at a cold turkey dinner, waiting for him to come home, which he never did. As a result, Christmastime for us is traumatic, opening doors to wounds from the past.

Mom fluttered her hands in the air, motioning for us to calm down. "But Alicia, those apartment buildings were in his name. Without a will, they'll go to his children."

"You've got it twisted around and dead wrong. The apartment buildings are in my name. My will stated that when I died, my son would inherit them. But now that he's gone, I'm changing my will."

My throat went dry. In a hoarse voice, I said, "We love you, Grandmother. We don't need to talk about this now. I'm just sad Dad died."

"That's right," Troy said, wiping his eyes. "I wish I'd been there to say goodbye to him before he passed away."

"Well, you weren't, and no one was. He died alone. I'll have you know."

I winced, imagining an awful end for my long-absent father.

Mom shook off the heavy yoke of sadness in the room and said, "Since you brought up the subject, tell us more about how you'll change your will."

Grandmother's voice was crisp and sharp as a knife. "Zane, my gardener, will inherit everything I own when I pass away."

Bile crept up my throat, and I swallowed hard.

Troy frowned and ran a hand through his hair.

Mom issued a silent scream and shook her fists in the air. She took a deep breath, just like she taught us when we were upset as kids, and said, "Your grandkids need that money. They don't have much, and they're trying to make their way in the world. Any gift you give would go a long ways toward helping them get ahead. It would be appreciated by all of us."

I leaned in. "It would."

"Yes," Troy said. "We'd really appreciate it."

"It's not my fault those two don't have much. They need to work harder, like their grandfather did. His work ethic and savvy investments are why I have so much. Like their father, they're lazy and waiting for money to fly into their bank accounts. Why don't you help them financially, if you feel that strongly? Oh, that's right, you don't have much, do you?"

Mom's face blazed bright red. "My family wasn't wealthy, like yours. We had to work hard for each dollar. But we know how to be happy and find joy in each moment. I'll help the kids make arrangements to fly down and see you. Instead of naming Zane to inherit everything, shouldn't it be family first?"

"He's been by my side the whole time, helping me. That's why I asked him to move into the house, so I could call him any time, in case I fell or needed something. Biff didn't want to be bothered with helping an old lady like me. He kept to himself, holed up in a dark apartment, ordering pizza deliveries and shuffling to the corner store for booze. His father and I were deeply disappointed in him. We paid for his Master's degree in Sociology and later learned he rarely attended classes, because he was partying too much. He never earned a dime from all the money we spent on his education. Francesca and Troy, don't be like your father. Make something of yourselves, because I won't be helping you."

Tears trickled down my cheeks. Dad said my grandmother was a cold-hearted witch, and he was right. Despite my growing dislike for my wealthy relative, I want to see her, change her mind and perhaps say a last goodbye to Dad.

Letting my gaze roam over my living room, I cleared my throat. "I'll let you know our travel arrangements. Are you sure we can't stay with you? It'd mean a lot to us, and we'd be there to offer you emotional support."

She cackled. "You're strangers to me, so don't bother coming. If you do, stay at a motel by the highway. I don't care if I see you. Goodbye."

I said, "I'm sorry about Dad, and thanks for letting us know. We'll see you soon."

But Grandmother had already hung up, and the only reply I heard was a dull dial tone.

With a sigh, I said to my mother and brother, "Well, that was a surprise."

Troy blew out a breath. "Merry Christmas, everyone."

Mom glared at my phone, as if it was the device's fault for ruining our evening. "You two need to go down there and convince her to put you in the will, not the gardener, whatever his name was."

"Zane," I said. "His name was Zane."

She flung her hands in the air. "Well, go meet him, check him out, see if he's conning the old lady."

Troy tilted his head. "Aren't you coming with us? It'd be easier that way."

"No, I can't. I've got a wedding to cater and another one after that. I wish I could fly down to support you, but I have too much going on to drop work and run off, ruining several someone's special days."

I nodded. Mom ran a catering business on a farm that held special events for rich people. For a short time, I worked for her, but I was fired when I dropped a tray of wine glasses, spilling red wine on a bride's white lace wedding dress. Before that, I tripped and splashed squash soup on a groom's tuxedo. Mom said I wasn't a good fit as an employee, and when I protested, she told me I was a risk to her livelihood. I had to go.

Now, I said, "I'll text my boss at the garden store and tell her Dad died, and I need time off. I'm sure it'll be no problem except I'll be short money this month."

Troy nodded. "I'll tell my boss too. He'll understand. If people need to wait in line longer for their coffee order at the bookstore, they can. It's not life and death."

Mom narrows her eyes. "She needs to name you in the will as her sole beneficiaries, but it sounds like she adores her gardener. We need a backup plan."

We tossed around ideas and came up with a contingency plan that will only come into play if it is the last resort. I didn't grow up to be a murderer, but if that's what I must do, I'll help my brother, and we'll make this upside-down situation right. Dad promised us riches, and we'll take back what was meant to be ours at any cost.

4

ZANE

I listened in on the conversation with her grandchildren and watched Alicia become more and more frustrated with each passing minute. She was right. They were money-hungry people, grabbing for any available scraps. They didn't sound at all sad about the news their dad had died. No one on the other end of the line sniffed or blew their nose into a tissue. No one wept in Washington State when Alicia relayed the horrible news that their loved one had passed away.

As the phone conversation continued, the tremor in Alicia's hands became markedly worse. I take my role as her helper seriously and when the call was almost over, I reached out, took the phone from her and hung up. If they kept talking, they'd only hear their own hot air blowing back in their faces.

I patted her cool hand, and she squeezed my fingers. I

said, "At least that's over with. Tomorrow, we'll let other people know."

She shrugged. "There's no one else to tell. No one cares about my son, not anymore. When he left and married that woman in Washington State, he burned bridges, and this town doesn't forget. They like to hold a grudge."

"What did he do, exactly, to offend people?"

"I don't want to talk about it now. That phone call really took the wind out of my sails. Will you help me get to bed?"

"I will. Would you like a heating pad or a hot water bottle to warm your feet?"

"Both, please. I'm so glad you're here, Zane. You're the only one who cares about me."

I brought over her walker and helped her up from a chair, staying by her side as she shuffled her way to the bathroom and then to bed. She sat down on the edge of the mattress and wiped her brow. "It's been a big day for us, hasn't it? I'm worn out."

I helped her lean back, raised her legs and put her head on a pillow. She coughed. "Will you pull up the blanket and tuck me in? I'm too exhausted to do that."

I pulled up a heavy wool Hudson Bay blanket. "There you are. Do you need a sleeping pill tonight?"

She wrinkled her nose. "No, you know I don't like taking those. I'll be fine. Thank you, and please lock up the house before you go to bed."

I leaned down and gave her cheek a quick peck. "I will. Goodnight. See you in the morning."

I left her room and tromped downstairs, glancing around the opulent surroundings filled with elegant furniture, plush hand-knotted rugs and expensive paintings. After she's gone , I'll be relieved not to carry her downstairs and upstairs each morning and night. I'll live here in the house and hire landscapers to maintain the lush grounds. I'll retire, which tragically is something my mother and father didn't get to do. Years of working too hard brought them early deaths.

I opened French doors and stepped outside, looking up. Stars sparkled in a night sky. "Forgive me," I whispered to my dear departed parents.

All my work and training brought me to this moment, and I covet what she has. I'll help Alicia meet her final end, leaving me everything she has.

5
___

FRANCESCA

Troy drove from San Francisco airport, past the Presidio and north across the Golden Gate Bridge. While he whistled along the way, I worried about what was ahead of us. Air in the Bay Area was light and dry compared to where we lived. My brother, who earned a law degree in Seattle but returned to Barnacle Island to work at a bakery, was too happy for my liking, considering the dire consequences ahead of ending up unexpectedly poor. But I resisted the urge to squash down and stomp on his joy.

I massaged my temples, where a headache throbbed. The two airports we'd come through on Christmas day were full of cheery people, in a sharp contrast to my dark mood. I was also a bit ashamed of myself for caring more about the loss of our expected inheritance than the death of our dad.

I checked my phone. "Is our reservation at the motel off the highway with yellow stucco siding? Or the white painted one by a pond?"

"The pond, it's closer to Grandma's."

"You mean Grandmother's, don't you?" We both laughed, but the tension of the day's travels made my jaw ache from gritting my teeth, and it was only early afternoon.

I gnawed on a cuticle and worried about honing my persuasive skills. I needed to up my game to convince Grandmother to ditch Zane and write us into the will. But we're family and that should matter most to her.

I turned off the radio. "What'll you do with the money, if she gives you an apartment building? Would you move into it, like Dad did?"

He pursed his lips, mulling this over. As if I haven't reviewed this question a gazillion times before in my mind, I said, "Would you start your own law practice?"

He tipped his head back and laughed. "I wouldn't do that. I went to law school because I was curious and wanted to learn about how the law works. But then I realized I didn't want to do that for work. Case closed."

I rolled my eyes. "So, the money? If she gives you some?"

Without hesitation, he says, "I'd buy the bakery and work for myself. That's my dream job."

"Come on, getting up at three in the morning and working until seven at night? You want to do that?"

He shrugged. "Better than working at a law firm night and day and on weekends. I met an associate who bought a condo and purchased furniture but he never had time to unpack it. His place was bare. He quit to live in a cabin on Hood Canal. I won't let myself get hooked into that grueling lifestyle. What about you?"

My mind drifted to Zane and the lifestyle of serving the rich as their servant, gardener and health aid. "We shouldn't be too hard on Zane. Maybe he means well and is helping Grandma."

Troy chuckled. "And pigs fly. But what would you do with the money?"

I took a deep breath. "I'd donate it to an animal rescue organization and adopt a kitten or a puppy or maybe both and give them a good home."

He cocked his head, giving me the side eye, looking like I'm crazy, and maybe I am. He said, "No, you'd do something different, I know you would. What do you want to bet Zane is a greedy gold digger, ready to off Grandma for his benefit?"

"Let's reserve judgement until we meet him. He might not have ulterior motives."

My brother turned off 101 and headed toward a two-story motel. A lone palm tree leaned, leaves swaying in a soft warm breeze.

I said, "Let's drop off our bags and go see Grandma and ask to see Dad's place. Maybe he left us something or wrote us letters he never sent."

Troy parked in a paved parking spot near a busy six-lane highway. "Don't get your hopes up."

A man with long hair jogged past, his arms pumping hard. He yelled, "Watch out, life forms on the asteroid are coming for us. Hide."

I shrugged and smirked at my brother. Who knew what was ahead? I didn't have a crystal ball for looking into the future, but I wish I did.

6

ALICIA

Birds chirping woke me in the morning, and I blinked. Sunshine peeked through the window blinds. I sighed. Although I had days and perhaps years left on this planet, my only son was gone. If only he hadn't been so selfish, thinking only of himself after he moved home. I'd hoped he'd visit me often and help me, but he didn't.

With a groan, I reached over and rang a bell by my bed.

Zane called from downstairs, "Coming. Be right there."

He came into my bedroom and helped me sit up in bed. Holding onto the edge of the mattress, I let my head adjust to sitting up. The room spun, and I blew out a breath. "The dizzies are back this morning."

He patted my shoulder. "Stay and get your bearings.

Don't get up too soon. I don't want you falling like you did the other day." He moved the walker over to me and waited, hands in front.

I gripped the cold metal walker, which resembled my hard barren life lacking warmth. The people I loved, my son and husband, died, leaving me alone. Gritting my teeth, I refused to surrender to self-pity. Everyone suffers loss. It's the human condition.

I said, "It's a good thing you're here. I don't know what I'd do without you. What are we doing today?"

Zane tilted his head. "Well, you didn't want to celebrate Christmas today, so soon after your son passed away, so I thought we'd take a nice drive and head to the beach. We can sit in the car, smell salt air and watch waves crash on the shore. We might see some surfers too."

I swallowed bitter tears for the loss of my son. "That's a good plan. Did those grandkids call to say if they're coming?"

"Yes, they'll be here in a few hours."

I scowled. "They never showed up before but now that their father died, they flew here to beg for money. We'll keep our own schedule and go to the beach. If they show up and find no one here, it's their own fault."

A flicker of a smile passed across Zane's face, but he wiped it away.

I said, "Help me up. I need to go to the bathroom. And thank you for all you do for me."

7

ZANE

Alicia hobbled into the bathroom and shut the door. She's avoided using adult diapers, but she's not far from that one-way aging cliff. I saw it with my extended relatives, when I wasn't out on a job pruning and raking. First was a walker, then adult diapers, followed by an event, such as a fall or a fire, and ending with a funeral casket or urn for the ashes. When I accepted Alicia's offer to move in and help her, she was alone. It'd be a shame for her to die and leave millions to thankless unseen relatives.

The toilet flushed, and I opened the blinds, letting light flood into the room. I put my hands on my hips and sighed, scanning the grounds. I wanted a life of my own and a love to cherish and spend Christmas with, but instead I'm trapped with an old lady, biding my time until her death. I've entered a strange bubble, where time is warped, and Alicia and I are both poised waiting for her death.

The bathroom door opened, and Alicia shuffled out, with a smile on her face and her white hair brushed. I strode over and helped her hobble to the top of the stairs.

"Ready?" I said.

"Go ahead."

I picked her up and carried her down the steps, wondering how many more times my back and spirit can take this. I've considered hastening the process of her greeting a final end, where she'd fall down the stairs or drown in a bath. But my conscience won't let me do that.

I placed her in a wheelchair waiting at the bottom of the stairs and went back up for the walker. I suggested she buy two of them, one for each floor of the massive house, but she didn't want to spend the money and said it was unnecessary.

She frowned, made a fist and thumped on the wheelchair arm. "Save money whenever you can. You never know when you'll need it."

I carried the walker down to the first floor. Surely, she won't live another year. I've suspended my life to be in service to her, but the sacrifice will be worth it in the end. My parents would be proud of me, if they were alive. This is the work they trained me to do. Bow down, hold your tongue and good things will come.

8

FRANCESCA

I grabbed my bag from the car and yawned. This morning, I woke to a screeching alarm at five, and it was dark when my brother Troy picked me up and drove to Seattle, navigating through thick clots of traffic to SeaTac airport.

I followed my brother, who had a spring in his step, toward the motel. Troy is a Golden Retriever, always ready for a new adventure. The motel was worn and built ninety or more years ago, but the price was right and it was near Grandma's place, nestled in the chichi town of Mill Valley. The other places cost too much for us. A room in a boutique hotel near the Sweetwater music venue cost more than I make in a month.

Swallowing tears, I recalled how Grandma rebuffed us and didn't want us staying with her. Only a cruel person would reject our overtures at friendliness on the day our dad died.

Troy marched to the motel front counter, letting the door slap shut in my face, which is how I've felt since last night, when the shocking call ended our quiet Christmas Eve celebration. Grandma snuffed out our holiday joy with her news, imparted in icy tones. Growing up, I doubted my Dad's version of her was true, but last night she sounded like an old woman with a cold, hard heart. I wanted to work tricks to warm her, so the family freeze ends and we'll get written into the will.

I stopped in the motel lobby and glanced around, massaging my temples. Tinny holiday tunes blasted through the room. Dark wood paneling on the walls meant we stepped into a time warp. A jolly man with rosy cheeks behind the counter wore a red Santa hat with white fur.

He scratched his forehead, told my brother where to sign and handed us two keycards. Troy waved, and we moved down a plaid carpeted hallway to our room with two double beds.

Troy said, "Just like when we were little kids, sharing a room."

I chuckled and told myself to snap out of my zombie state. I had to be sharp for when we saw Grandma. Coffee might bring out my polite, persuasive side, but all I wanted to do was crash on the floral bedspread, take a nap and forget my father passed away. Dad was the source of our troubles, and this was his fault, but we'd make it right.

9

TROY

We checked into an older motel near Highway 101 and grabbed two key cards. Holiday music jingled and jangled in the background, and a stout man at the front desk pointed out the free coffee bar in the lobby. But all Francesca and I wanted to do was drop our bags in the room and head over to see our grandmother. The front desk man called, "Merry Christmas! It's good you're here to see your grandma. She'll like that."

In the room, we threw our bags on the beds, used the restroom and headed to the car. My sister lagged behind, whining about wanting to get a cup of coffee, but I said, "We don't have time for that. Grandma's waiting for us."

As I drove, my thoughts drifted to growing up on an island without a dad. It wasn't easy, but I made it through. Dad called the day I turned eighteen and told me about the apartment building gift that would change my life. That's when I decided I could afford to go to law school, if I got in. I could do whatever I liked, because a pot of gold was waiting for me at the end of death's rainbow. Dad said it was a sure thing, but to my horror, he did nothing to cinch it down and make it our reality.

I gritted my teeth. We needed to get into his apartment to search for a will. Perhaps he misplaced it and forgot to file the paperwork. Maybe he left it under a couch cushion. Aretha Franklin's handwritten will was found in a couch cushion after her death and ruled valid by a jury, so we might find Dad's will tucked away.

I frowned. Grandma might have found Dad's will and ripped it up, because she wanted to leave the apartment buildings to Zane, the interloper.

Clearing my throat, I said to my sister, "We need to separate Grandma from this gardener, so he doesn't influence her while we're there."

Francesca yawned and covered her mouth, like Dad taught us. Although he was raised in a wealthy household, we grew up lower middle-class.

Francesca nodded. "I totally agree. We'll divide and conquer. I can tell Zane is a bad influence. We need to shut him up or send him out to buy coffees."

I drove past a closed coffee shop. "It's Christmas day, so not much is open."

"We can tell him to take a break and go for a drive in

Grandma's car. Remember that big black shiny boat of a car she had when we last saw her?"

"It was huge. She had a chauffeur driving her around, while she sat in the back seat." We laughed, and I said, "Maybe she still has it."

Francesca tilted her head. "She's tight-fisted with money, Dad said."

I turned down a narrow street and winced at my financial situation. Based on the assumption that Dad told the truth, and I'd be rich one day, I racked up a ton of student loan debt. But now it looked like he was a liar to his only son. I wiped tears from my eyes.

Francesca wrinkled her nose. "The motel soap was perfumy, like an old lady smell."

"We're about to see an old lady, so get ready. We'll endure the iceberg, as Dad put it, so we can soften her up. I'm not looking forward to this."

She said, "Me neither. "But wait, is that her car coming out of her estate? The guy driving looks about our age. I bet she's with him. Follow that car.

I turned and followed the black sedan. With a frown, I said, "I don't get it. I asked them to be home when we arrived. What's so important they couldn't wait?"

10

———

ZANE

I helped Alicia climb in the back seat and buckled up her seatbelt. Trotting to the driver's side, I slid in and started the car, pushing a button to open the estate gates.

My pulse picked up, because we were running late. It had taken Alicia longer than usual to eat breakfast and wash up and shuffle out to the car that I washed yesterday. I wanted to leave before the greedy grandchildren arrived. Troy called on the house landline, and I answered, hearing their travel plans, but I didn't relay the information to Alicia.

Black wrought iron gates slowly slid open. My palms grew cold. The blood-sucking leeches of grandchildren ready to attach themselves to my elderly charge were due here any minute. They didn't pay attention to her until now, but I've been by her side for many years. I'll take her to the beach and ensure I'm the only one named in her new will.

Putting the car in gear, I glided out to a side street and pushed a button to close the black gates. Blowing out a breath, I drove away and wiped my brow. But I glanced in the rear-view mirror and swallowed hard. A white sedan that might be a rental car with two people in it paused at the front gates and followed us.

I tapped on the steering wheel and drummed out a beat of pure panic. "How about we'll go to Rodeo Beach?"

Alicia smiled in the back seat. "Whatever you think is best. You're in charge."

I took a circuitous route on side roads, trying to lose the white car that was tailing us. A car horn honked. Two people rolled down their windows and waved and yelled, but I carried on and drove ahead, turning up the music in the car and drowning out their cries.

Alicia nodded and closed her eyes. "Yes, I love Mozart. That's just the right music for a day like today. It's Christmas, but I lost my son, and he's gone forever."

Tears slid down her wrinkled cheeks, and she wiped them away, letting out a sigh.

I turned right and entered a dark tunnel leading to the public beach. She needed company and someone to look after her. I wouldn't let the grandkids swoop in and hurt her feelings, by taking money and leaving again. She needed a protector and caregiver, and I was the man for the job.

I drove down a two-lane paved road and followed a meandering river, passing meadows. Turning down the music, I said, "No flowers out today."

Alicia nodded. "I love those little yellow flowers that pop up, but they're gone now. I don't know if I'll live to see them again in the spring."

I waved a hand in front of my face. "You're healthy for your age, and you've got something to live for. We'll see the yellow flowers together in April."

Her face sagged. "I'm not sure I want to hold on. There's not much to live for, if it's only the sight of yellow flowers keeping me going. I'm just an old lady with no one left."

I glanced in the rear-view mirror and smiled. "But I'm here. Come on, cheer up. It's Christmas, and the Market delivered a special dinner I'll heat up this afternoon, with turkey and stuffing and mashed potatoes and those dinner rolls you like."

She brightened in the back seat. "I do like those rolls, you're right. All right, I'll hang in there and won't give up. Not yet."

A wide sandy beach appeared ahead of us. Frothing white-capped waves pounded on the surf, kicking up sea spray. Gesturing to the magnificent display of the Northern California coast, I said, "And here we are, right where we need to be on Christmas Day. I'll park in a handicapped spot, and you can roll down your window and breathe the salt air."

She bit her lip. "My husband loved to come here. I miss him so much, and I'll see him soon."

I cringed at her death wish and parked, hanging a handicapped parking sign from the rear-view mirror. Alicia rolled down her window, took a deep breath and smiled. I leaned back in my seat and frowned.

The white sedan with two passengers about the right age to be Alicia's grandchildren entered the parking area and crept toward us. My chest tightened. I didn't want Alicia to deal with a confrontation, not after having just dealt with calling the crematorium yesterday to cart away her son's body. She deserved a day of peace and quiet after her angst and loss.

I started the car and crept forward. Alicia said in a gravelly voice, "Why are we leaving? I want to stay longer. We only just got here."

The white sedan turned and stopped in front of me, blocking us in.

With a sigh, I braked. Here we go, I thought. Those kids are going to swarm out of the car like angry bees, but I won't let them sting Alicia. She means well, even though she can be crusty and cold at times. They don't know her like I do, and they haven't seen her kinder, gentler side, which swoops by every so often, like a rare comet.

11

———

FRANCESCA

We drove up to my grandmother's house, and I pointed, nudging my brother, who was driving. "Look, she's leaving. The gates are closing, and they're driving away. Follow them."

Troy hunched over the wheel, frowning. "I bet that groundskeeper didn't tell her we were coming. I knew I couldn't trust him."

Patting his arm, I shook my head. "Maybe something important came up. Like she suddenly had to go to church, because she's upset Dad died."

"She didn't sound that upset about it yesterday."

I said, "I was pretty broken up, despite not seeing him for years. It's just the thought of not having a father, you know? It's like a limb was cut off, one I didn't use, but still, I notice it's missing."

Troy took a sharp turn, following a shiny black car. "I felt like that too, and still do. Man, that guy isn't making it easy for me to stay behind him. He's ignoring us on purpose. Let's roll down the windows and wave our hands to flag them down. I want to see Grandma."

I rolled down my window, yelled to the car ahead and waved my hands, but the black car didn't slow down. Troy did that same and shrugged. Air whipped past, smelling of eucalyptus trees.

I took a deep breath and rolled up my window. "What now?"

"We follow them to where they're going and when they stop, we confront them about ditching us."

I shook my head. "Not everything has to be about conflict."

"But it is."

I made a face. "Maybe that's why you don't have a girl-friend. You don't have to win every argument, like you did when we were kids."

He ran a hand through his hair and stopped at a light. "Yeah, you're right. It's an old habit and hard to break."

I pointed. "They're going into a tunnel. Follow them."

"I can't. I have to wait for the light."

We waited in silence, and the light changed. Driving into the long, dark tunnel, he said, "It's not just me who was wounded from how we grew up. You're alone, but you'd like a partner. Am I right?"

Coming out into sunlight and leaving the tunnel of truths behind, I exhaled slowly. "It's true. I'd like to be with someone, but I haven't found the right person yet. Maybe I'm too picky. I'm afraid of someone becoming close and then leaving me."

"Me too. Like when Dad left."

A river appeared on our left, and Troy continued on a two-lane road, making our way to the ocean. I said, "And that marks the end of our impromptu counselling session. We're going to the beach Dad took us to when we were little, remember that?"

Troy smiled. "That was fun, running in the waves."

"Until a wave carried me out."

"And Dad rescued you."

Ahead of us, the shiny black car parked in the lot. I rolled my window down and took a deep breath of briny sea air. The car with Grandma moved ahead, I said, "Stop them. We've got to see Grandma. Block them off."

Troy turned the steering wheel and stopped in front of the black car, blocking them in. He cringed. "What if Grandma isn't in the car? Maybe her chauffeur went out for a drive by himself. We should've rung the bell at her house. We jumped to conclusions and assumed she was leaving."

I wagged an index finger at him. "But we know what she's like. And we know he's a greedy gardener who manipulated her into giving him everything. He probably set up this trip to keep her away from us. Let's go."

We jumped out of the car, slamming the doors. Wind whipped past, and I shivered in the cool Christmas day San Francisco area weather. Goosebumps rose on my arms and legs, exposed in my shorts and t-shirt.

Inhaling a deep breath of salt air, I strode over to the black car and knocked on the driver's side window.

12

ZANE

I braked to a stop and clenched the steering wheel, fuming. A white car blocked the road ahead of me. A line of parked cars on my left gave me no room to turn around, and to my right was a wide sandy beach and the Pacific Ocean. Short of sprouting water wings, we had no way out.

Two people jumped out of the white car and strode toward us, clenching their hands. Curly brown hair of a woman in her mid-thirties whipped around in the wind. A man about her age ran a hand through his short sandy hair. They marched in unison, and I sucked in a breath, seeing the striking resemblance to the woman in the back seat.

Alicia said, "What's going on? Who are those people?"

Two people knocked on the driver's window, and I gulped. They looked angry, and I avoided confrontations.

I said to my passenger, "I think your grandchildren have arrived."

She swatted a hand in the air. "Tell them not to interrupt me. I was enjoying my time at the beach until they showed up."

I rolled the window down and feigned ignorance. "Yes, can I help you?"

The woman who must be Francesca leaned in and looked toward the back seat. "Grandmother, we came to see you. Can we get in the back seat and talk?"

"No, don't bother me. I'm having a quiet time, grieving by myself."

Troy said, "We'll wait right here until you agree to see us."

Cars honked to get through the blocked road. I pointed and said, "You'd better move your car before it gets towed. And you'd better do what your grandmother says. She needs time alone today."

Troy moved away, but Francesca's feet were planted firmly in place, with her hands at her sides. She said, "I'm sorry we didn't call or write or send cards. Dad told us not to. He said unkind things about you and colored our views. I apologize. I should've ignored him and reached out to get to know you. But we can do that now."

Troy parked the white car and came over, furrowing his brows. He looked just like his father, and I was surprised Alicia didn't spot that right away. But her eyesight was failing and she had reasons to be distracted today.

Alicia sniffed. "It's too late for that. Go walk on the beach and leave me be."

Francesca said, "It's not too late. Can I join you in the back?"

I locked the car doors with a click. Francesca tried to open the back door, but the door handle didn't budge. She knocked on the smoky glass back window. "Please, let me in."

She didn't get a reply, so she inched over to my open window. She spoke too close to my face, and I turned away, smelling ketones on her breath. She needed to eat something or drink coffee, because I suspected she was running on empty. If she took a swig of mouth wash, she'd spare the rest of us from her horrible halitosis.

"Grandmother, I love you, and I'd like to get to know you better, if you'd let me."

Silence reigned from the queen of ice in the back seat, and I waited for what would happen next. This wasn't my circus on the day after her son's death. She celebrated Christmas, and I'd wanted to make this a special day for her.

Troy pushed his sister aside. "Grandma, we'd like to get into Dad's apartment. Maybe he left a small token of his love for us there. Would you please give us the key?"

After a beat, Alicia said, "Fine, I'll tell Zane to let you

in, but he'll watch every move you make. You have no right to your father's things."

A tear slid down Troy's cheek. "But he promised he'd leave me his chess set when he died."

"That's gone, but you can look through the rest of his belongings and take one thing each. The rest is mine. I paid for the place where he lived, after all. He was supposed to outlive me by many years, but look what happened."

"Now, now," I said. "I don't want you to get upset. It's not good for your heart."

Troy and Francesca exchanged a quick look. Troy said, "I'm sorry to hear about your heart. Can we at least bring dinner and share Christmas dinner together, after we see Dad's place?"

Alicia shrugged. "That will be fine. Now go run and play at the beach. Clean your shoes before you show up at my house in one hour. But leave me alone until then."

The two grandchildren grinned. Francesca said, "I'm looking forward to it."

Troy nodded. "Great, see you then."

They ran off to the beach, hair flying in the stiff breeze and laughing, like two little kids. I bit my lip, snuffed out a growing ember of jealousy and said, "You're not seriously going to entertain them tonight, are you? I thought the idea was to keep them at a distance."

Alicia said, "Let's not talk for a while. Take me back to

that other parking spot. You've been kind to me, but what I do with my family is my own business."

A chill swept over me, and I shuddered at the thought of losing everything I'd hoped for and planned on. I'd worked as her aid for little pay, free accommodations and a heavy burden of being on call twenty-four-seven with no vacation time.

"Yes, ma'am, whatever you say."

13

ALICIA

Zane parked in my preferred spot, and I rolled down my window, letting the breeze swish past. I won't let my sniveling grown grandkids muscle their way into my life, but it's Christmas, and they deserve to share it with family.

I wiped a tear from my cheek and inhaled sea air. I knew what it was like to be alone on a holiday, from my life before I married my husband. All I could afford was a bowl of oatmeal for Christmas dinner, and I ate it in my cold apartment, accompanied by a family of sturdy cockroaches. I'd tried to banish them, but they wouldn't leave, so I grew to accept my permanent skittering guests.

I scanned the beach and saw the two racing down the beach barefoot, tagging each other. Francesca was right. Her father didn't like me one bit, and he made it his mission to poison everyone else who entered his orbit.

Everyone was sucked into his views and believed him, except for his ex-wife. She had a good head on her shoulders.

I closed the window, shut out the wind and banished thoughts about my son to the other side of the ocean. He wasn't worth wallowing in grief or losing sleep. He was a dud from the beginning, when he wouldn't talk until he was four, making me ashamed in front of my friends.

"Drive, Zane. Let's go home."

He nodded, and the car started, creeping forward, like my life in my later years. Time has slowed and every day takes a year. How unfair that days flip by in a millisecond as a youth, but they stretch on, yawning as if for years, the longer I live.

I turned and gave the beach a last look. I may have misjudged those two and been jaded by my son's views. They might be interesting people to get to know after all. Maybe I'll leave them a snippet of something in my revised will.

Zane glanced in the rear-view mirror. "Pardon me, what did you just say about the will?"

"Did I say something out loud? I was just mumbling to myself. Nothing to worry about. You'll still get the bulk of my estate. You deserve it after having worked so hard for me. Have I ever said thank you?"

"Not often, ma'am. It's rare to hear it, to be honest."

"Well, thank you, Zane. Thank you very much for keeping me afloat with your many miraculous efforts."

He beamed.

"Later today, see if you can find a way to turn our dinner for two into supper for four."

In the rear-view mirror, I saw him glower for an instant before wiping the look from his face. I turned to look out the window at the meandering river as we passed by and a feeling of cold caution crawled over my skin. I'd watch him and make sure he didn't take advantage of me. Since my call to Francesca last night, he'd grown slightly cantankerous, as if he was entitled to my millions, and that wasn't right. It was my gift to give to anyone I designated as a beneficiary.

He hunched over the wheel, jaw clenched, staring straight ahead. He grimaced, and a wave of anger rose up from the front seat, sweeping over me. I shuddered, as a violent image of Zane picking me up and tossing me off a cliff, into the sea, flashed through my mind.

He looked up, and we locked eyes in the rear-view mirror. He cleared his throat. "Would you like to go through town to see the Christmas decorations?"

I swallowed bitter bile. The holiday wasn't working out the way I'd hoped. Not at all. "No, let's go home. I'm tired and want to take a nap."

14

FRANCESCA

Chasing my brother on a sandy beach, I tagged him and tackled him, and we collapsed on the sand, breathing hard. I said, "Too much has happened since Christmas Eve. My head is spinning."

He nodded and wiped sweat from his brow with the back of his hand. "The three of us should get together more often. Barnacle Island isn't that big."

I sighed. "But we're all so busy."

He looked at me. "But we're not too busy to see family. Let's not end up like Dad."

I half-smiled. "That'll be our mantra, let's not end up like Dad. He was the example of what not to be. Don't do what Dad did and avoid your family."

Troy gazed at the pounding waves slamming onto a sandy shore. Out in the water, surfers sat on surfboards or paddled out farther. He said, "He died alone, which is so sad."

"I know. What a horrible way to go. Ready to go back?"

"Yeah, race you to the car."

Wind whipped through my hair, and our bare feet pounded on hard sand by the surf's edge. White foaming waves crept toward my toes, and I scurried away, wishing I was a carefree child again.

Salty ocean mist blew in my eyes, and I tipped back my head, laughing, and Troy did the same. For an instant in time, we were innocent kids, not two mature adults ready to blot out our grandmother's life to benefit our own.

15
____

TROY

We grabbed the sneakers we'd left on the beach and ran to the car. I let my older sister get there first, because holidays always got her down, ever since Dad left us. Heaped on top of the gray, dreary weather this time of year back home on Barnacle Island, was the news Dad died, our grandmother's frigid tone and the fact that we were to inherit nothing. It was all too much.

Francesca slapped the rental car hood with a hand. "I win."

I smiled. "You're always faster than me."

She eyed me. "Wait a minute, did you let me win? Don't do that."

I focused on brushing sand off my feet and putting on my shoes, tying the laces. "Nope, I'd never do that."

We climbed in the car and left the beach Dad took us

to when we were young. I blew out a breath. "Being back there was a trip back in time, with crabby granny in the back seat of the black car, the sullen driver and the amazing waves. This is a lot to take in, isn't it?"

She pouted, crossed her arms and was silent.

Driving by a river, I headed for the tunnel. "Hey, Franny, let me know if you get depressed and this is too much, okay?"

She didn't answer, so I slowed the car and stared at her. "I mean it. I don't want you going to a sad place. Tell me early on, and I'll do whatever it takes to keep you from spiraling down."

She looked over at me with tears in her eyes. "I'm aware of the risks I took coming here. My feelings about Dad abandoning us means I have triggers, but I'm handling them better. Or I thought I was, until now. Grandmother is cold as ice, and I feel like a kid around her, totally helpless."

I drew a deep breath and pondered my emotionally tender weather vane of a sister. She protected me when we were young by taking on sadness for both of us. When I graduated from law school, I moved home to take care of her for a change. She was stuck in the wrinkled bowels of the past, but I wanted her to move on. So far, I haven't made much progress with Project Francesca, but I can't tell her how to view the world or demand she switch her filter from dark and depressing to rose-tinted glasses.

Going through the tunnel, I was quiet and waited for

her to open up. We came out on the other side, and I blinked in brilliant sunlight. I grinned. "I forgot to bring my sunglasses. I hope our future's so bright, we'll have to wear shades."

She said in a soft voice, "I hope so."

I turned down a road and tried to boost her mood. Ticking off items to accomplish on the fingers of my right hand, I said, "Okay, here's our plan. We'll stop at Grandma's, pick up the butler chauffeur gardener guy, go through Dad's things searching for a hidden will and a token item to remember him by. Then we'll buy food and end up at Grandma's for dinner. How's that sound?"

Francesca groaned and rubbed her eyes, which was not the response I wanted. I'd hoped to distract her from her internal potential storm of bad feelings.

She said, "I hardly slept last night after Grandma called, with so many thoughts running through my mind. I need to take a nap."

My mouth dropped open, and I braked at a stop light. "But we don't have time for that."

She stretched her arms. "Can't we stop at the motel for twenty minutes? That's all I need."

I gripped the wheel tight. I didn't want to be late to see our battle axe of a grandmother. In a gentle tone of voice, I said, "At the beach, Grandma showed signs of softening her mood toward us. We need to keep the momentum going, and I don't want to be late. That'd tick her off.

We've got to win her over to our side, so she'll ditch the gardener and write us into the will."

"Fine, just stop at the motel so I can wash the sand off my feet,"

I turned the car away from Grandma's and steered toward the dated motel by the highway. Letting out a sigh, I wished I could wave a wand over my sister's mood, transforming her into a happy person. She deserved to have a wonderful life, especially on Christmas day, and I'd do my best to deliver that.

16

───────

FRANCESCA

Inside the motel room, I flopped on the bed and groaned. Troy was all energy and purpose, bustling around, washing his feet in the bathroom. I just wanted to rest and shut out thoughts about my odd, extended family. Sleep would wash away negative feelings inside.

I drifted off, until Troy clapped his hands. "Chop, chop, Franny. Let's go."

I opened my eyes, feeling a bit better for the break from reality of feeling unloved by my grandmother on Christmas. I sat up and brushed hair from my eyes. "Fine," I grumbled, getting up and lumbering to the bathroom. "Give me a minute, and I'll be ready."

A few minutes later, Troy knocked on the door. "It's time. We've got to go. Are you ready?"

I stuck my feet under the faucet in the tub, ran the

water, washed off sand and drowned out my brother's words. He meant well, but he was overbearing at times, especially since he came home after law school.

He rapped hard on the door and wiggled the knob. "Time's up."

"Coming," I said, drying my feet with a towel. I whipped the door open and grinned. "Let's go. What're you waiting for?"

I slipped on my sneakers and strode to the door, gathering courage to face the grueling time ahead at Dad's place, where he died, and over a holiday meal with my aloof grandmother. I'd rather be home, snug in my apartment, wrapped in a blanket and nursing a cup of cocoa, but life threw cold water in my face and this was my new reality.

Following Troy out of the room, I nodded to myself. We had to convince Grandma we meant well. Like a spigot in the bathtub. I wanted her to turn on the money tap, release me from being poor and know I'd be rich when she passed away.

Climbing in the car, Troy drove out of the parking lot, but I said, "I left my purse with my hair brush at the motel. I have to go back to get it."

He pressed his lips together and turned the car around. "Fine, go get it. But make it fast. We've got to be on time."

17

ZANE

The sky was blue, sunshine shone bright, but at the estate, my mood was dark. I helped the old lady get into bed and pulled down the blinds in her room. I trotted down the stairs and frowned. She shouldn't have told the grandchildren I'd be their guide when they looked around their father's apartment. I work for her, not them. It was bad enough yesterday being in the stuffy apartment with a dead body until the mortuary workers arrived.

I rubbed my aching neck. Alicia shot me darts with negative looks on the way home. I'm worn out from working long hours each day and being at her beck and call. These two people flew in, and they're poised to take, take, take, but I've slaved away for their relative. They are mercenary and motivated by money, with pretend fake pleasant voices cooing at Alicia near the beach, but all they want is her money. I know what that smells like, because I'm the same way, but I cover it up better. My father taught me to be polite and obsequious.

I went in the kitchen and brewed myself a coffee, using the new machine, and sat facing the grounds I maintain. But the bitter brew tasted off, and I scowled, setting down the cup. I needed a plan to keep them from fawning on Alicia and winning her over.

Water in the swimming pool glimmered in the sun, offering a simple solution, and I nodded. The grandkids will drown, and I'll tell the police they were drunk and went swimming. But I'll hold their heads under and help them along the last mile. I'll add sleeping pills to their drinks before I do the deed. No one will be the wiser, and I'll protect what's meant to be mine.

18

FRANCESCA

We arrived at Grandma's place, and I hopped out, ringing a buzzer, but the black gates didn't swing open. A man's voice came through a speaker. "Wait out there," he said, "I'll join you."

He hurried out of the house, closed the door behind him and strode out through a side gate. Putting a finger to his lips, he said, "Your grandmother's sleeping, and she needs to rest. We'll go in your car. I'll show you where your father lived."

My stomach knotted, picturing where Dad died, but I tamped down my queasy feelings. I wanted to go through his things and see if he left a note or a treasure for me. Maybe I'd find his will. My brother would look up to me, like he did when we were kids, and I'd be a hero.

I gestured to the car, where Troy waited at the wheel,

his jaw clenched. "Why don't you sit up front and give directions? I'll get in back."

He nodded. "That'll be fine."

I nodded, thinking he was a stiff, formal creature, but then again he was Grandmother's servant and hired help. Maybe he thought it was best to keep a distance between staff and family. He was about our age, with curly brown hair cut short.

We climbed in the car, and I buckled up in back. Sniffing the air, I detected the faint odor of baby powder coming off the gardener. I shrugged. Maybe he smelled like that from working for and helping the old lady.

Zane pointed and told Troy to back out of the driveway, go straight ahead, then go right and turn left.

I leaned forward. "How long have you worked for my grandma?"

He paused a beat. "I grew up on the property. My parents worked for your grandparents for many years."

Something in the weight of his words and intonation made me tilt my head, but I couldn't see his face to read anything into it. Was he resentful? He shouldn't be. After all, Grandmother said she'd leave everything she had to him. I smiled to myself and looked down, not wanting Zane to see my eyes. My brother and I were about to change Grandma's plans and cut the gardener out. He just didn't know it yet.

Troy glanced over. "Do your folks still live there?"

He shook his head. "No, sadly, they passed away."

A heavy silence filled the car. We passed big old gnarled trees and turned onto Miller Avenue, lined with stores. A high-school kid wearing a helmet blasted past us on the right side of the road, gunning his electric bike.

In a bitter voice, Zane said, "My folks never had a day off in all the years they worked there. Their bodies wore out. I think that's why they died early."

I cringed, as the thought crossed my mind that my grandparents might've been cruel inconsiderate rich snobs under a veneer of polished public personas. "I'm sorry to hear that. It's so sad."

Zane craned his neck to look at me. "I've never had a day off either, to be honest, since I started working there. I'm supposed to be living in the cottage, but I sleep in a bed upstairs in a backroom, so your grandmother can call for me anytime, day or night."

I said, "That sounds awful. You're working really hard. No wonder Grandmother wants to leave you something in her new will."

Zane said, "Actually, she's leaving me everything, like she told you last night when she called."

My chest tightened. My brother and I exchanged a quick panicked look in the rear-view mirror. We couldn't let that happen.

Zane pointed ahead. "Take a left in one block at the light. We'll walk up to an apartment building by a creek. Your father liked to look out at it."

He turned to me, furrowing his dark brown eyebrows.

"Let's be clear about what your grandmother intends to do. She'll draw up a new will when the holiday is over and leave everything to me. You two haven't been around, but I've taken care of all her needs for years. You can't just pop in when it suits you, expecting to grab money and run back home."

I chewed on the inside of my cheek. I hadn't expected the gardener to have a backbone and defend himself. I thought he'd be a meek, mild-mannered man, bowing down to Grandma and the strong, silent type with us. But this guy had guts. He was fending off attacks and shutting us down before we had a chance to launch our plan.

Troy said, "Our father promised us those buildings. We have a right to come down here and take back what was to be ours."

Zane said, "Park over there. We'll walk up to the building."

Troy parked by the curb, and traffic swished past. I shook off the strange aggressive vibes from our car ride and climbed out of the car on the sidewalk side.

Zane pointed. "He lived up there."

I looked up at a brown shingled building with white trim, where Dad died. Tall redwood trees towered over it, providing shade on a sunny day. I rubbed my forehead. Standing in the sun on Christmas day was surreal, not to mention having a dead Dad.

Troy patted my shoulder. "It's weird being here, isn't it?"

"Follow me," Zane said and walked up a drive. We tromped behind him, and I wondered what we'd find in Dad's apartment. I crossed my fingers and hoped we'd find a dusty will naming us as beneficiaries to the two buildings.

An ugly thought fluttered through my mind, and I made a face. Even if he had a will, it wouldn't make a difference, because Grandma had lived longer than him, against all odds. The buildings were in her name. She could do what she liked with them.

I frowned and marched ahead. I should give up hope for getting my promised inheritance, but I couldn't let it go. I'd held this vision of my future for years, and I had to wrestle it into fruition.

With a sinking feeling in my stomach, I plodded up a set of wooden steps. Zane held an exterior door open for me and gestured down a hallway. "After you."

I squinted in dim light and stepped inside.

"Which one is it?" I asked, hit with the realization that he had known my dad far better than I did near the end. Zane was the one holding my family together while he was Grandma's health aid and landscaper.

I tiptoed down a carpeted hall and wrinkled my nose, smelling cooked onions. Guilt stabbed me in my gut. Zane helped my father and my grandmother, while up north on Barnacle Island, I'd led a quiet, selfish life.

Zane stopped outside a door and held up a key. "This is the one."

He unlocked it and stepped aside. "You go first, but you might want to breathe through your mouth."

I sniffed the air and doubled over, gagging at the foul odor of recent death, rotting trash, cigarettes, cheap perfume and booze. Troy broke out coughing and trotted over to a window, throwing it open.

A breeze blew through, freshening the air, but the place still stank of regrets and things ignored for far too long.

Zane perched on a hard wooden chair and put his hands together. "Have a look around to see if there's anything you'd like to take to remember him by."

I shrugged. "He wasn't the best Dad, but we'll see. Thanks for letting us in."

Troy and I pushed cardboard pizza boxes aside. On impulse, I opened one and frowned at gray furry mold on shriveled slices. Slamming the box closed, I turned to a desk and examined overdue invoices for gas, electricity and water bills.

I said, "Looks like he wasn't worried about paying his bills."

Zane said, "He expected his mother to pay his bills, when he was in too deep. His pattern of behavior frustrated her, but he didn't change, even when she threatened to cut him off financially. He just carried on the same way, expecting hand-outs."

My face heated, because in a way, my brother and I are guilty of acting the same way. We're here to hop on Grandma's gravy train of money. A colorful greeting card on Dad's desk caught my attention, and I picked up a birthday card I sent him years ago. He'd propped it up and put it in a prominent place, so maybe it meant something to him. Or, maybe he hadn't gotten around to throwing it out.

Troy waved a piece of paper in the air. "Got something."

Just then, a woman with bleached blond hair in her late fifties pushed open the door, storming into the room. "Who are you? Where's Ted?"

19

ZANE

 blond woman burst in the room, yelling, and I jumped to my feet. "Don't come in here. This is off-limits to everyone but family."

She smiled, and her bright red lipstick glistened. She held up a key. "It's too late for that."

Troy ran a hand through his hair. "Who are you?"

She put a hand on her broad hip. "I'll ask the same. Who are you?"

Troy said, "I'm his son."

Francesca nodded. "I'm his daughter."

The blond frowned. "Where's Biff? I've been trying to reach him. He's not answering his phone."

Troy, Francesca and I shared a quick glance, and I nodded. I'd do the dirty work, like always, with no thanks. "You may want to sit down," I said.

She shook her head. "Tell me right now. I want to know."

I took a deep breath and dove in. "I'm sorry to tell you this, but he passed away yesterday afternoon."

Her mouth fell open, her face went pale, and she dropped her purse. I offered her my chair, but she swayed back and forth and slumped to the floor.

I patted the woman's cheeks, took her pulse, detecting a steady beat, and turned to the grandchildren. "She's out cold. Let's make her comfortable. She's got a pulse, and she's breathing."

I said to Francesca, "Get her a glass of water."

To Troy, I said, "Let's elevate her feet, put a blanket over her and put a pillow under her head."

They followed my orders, and soon, the woman blinked her eyes and touched her forehead. "What happened? Is Biff really dead? He promised to take me to Vegas next week."

A tear dribbled down her cheek, but I wasn't sure if it was due to Biff's death or her loss of an upcoming trip. "Just rest," I said, "and then you need to go home."

She sat up and burst into tears. "But he told me I could live here and not pay rent. I moved in yesterday morning and only left to spend Christmas Eve with my mother in Redding."

I shook my head. "The building is owned by his mother, and you need to leave."

The woman wailed. Tears ran down her cheeks,

leaving tracks in her makeup. "I have nowhere to go. My things are here."

She blubbered, shoulders shaking, and I finally caved. "Fine, you can sleep here tonight, but tomorrow you must be gone."

She sniffed and blew her nose on a tissue. "Thank you. Now if you'll all leave, I'd like to have some time to myself."

I studied the two grandchildren for their take on the situation, and they shook their heads.

Troy said, "Unless we have something in writing, we don't know she was really Dad's girlfriend. She could be using this as an excuse to come in and take what she likes. She might be taking advantage of us."

But I shook my head. "I believe her, and shame on you for judging her and leaving her out in the cold on Christmas. She can sit in the kitchen while you look through things and take what you want."

The blond woman's face flushed. "My things are mixed in with his. Don't take anything of mine."

"Please, go sit in the kitchen. I'll tell you when you can come out."

20

FRANCESCA

My head was light, and it had been too long since my last meal. The older blond had a key, so maybe she was telling the truth about being Dad's girlfriend. She lumbered into the kitchen, shoulders sagging with the weight of grief, and I turned to the squalor in the room. Papers were everywhere, tossed on the floor.

I sniffed the air, detecting cigarette smoke, and arched my eyebrows. When Dad lived with us, he didn't smoke. I picked up a stained coffee cup and frowned at cigarette butts inside.

Troy came over and said to me in a low voice, "I found this before she came in." He handed me a piece of paper with handwriting scrawled on it. I read: "To whom it may concern: In the event of my death, I bequeath all my earthly belongings and money to my dog Fifi."

Zane looked over from his chair and scowled, crossing his legs.

I said to Zane, "Did my dad have a dog?"

He nodded. "Yes, but it passed away a few years ago."

I shoved the useless piece of paper back in Troy's hands. "Let's keep looking. We don't have much time."

But fifteen minutes later, all I'd found were mismatched men's socks, a metal detector, the mandatory shorts and long white socks to go with that hobby, and a stack of old books. Opening one, I inhaled dust and sneezed, gently closing it. Dirty coffee mugs littered counter tops, as if he'd rather buy a new cup than wash one. Nothing reflected the brilliant mind Mom said he once had.

I turned to my brother. "Did you find anything?"

He raised a couch cushion, looked underneath and let it flop down. "Nope. He lived like a pig, and he was a fraud of a dad."

From the kitchen, the blond said, "Don't speak ill of the dead. He wasn't perfect, but no one is. He was a nice guy and generous with his money."

I asked Zane. "What about Dad's bank accounts? Who gets what's in those?"

Zane emitted a long sigh and shook his head, as if my brother and I were greedy, grubbing children with our hands out, wanting more, and I suppose we were.

He said, "You'll have to ask your grandmother who

was named as his beneficiaries, if she knows. The banks are closed for Christmas."

From the kitchen, Dad's girlfriend said, "He didn't have much, I know that."

Zane narrowed his eyes at me. "A man died, and yet you march in here, cold-heartedly searching for a will that doesn't exist. Shame on you. Don't you care about the man he was?"

I let his words sink in, my eyes roaming over shelves in the living room. I swallowed tears and said, "He left us without a word and was a dark blot in our lives. We moved on. I don't need to know more about a father who abandoned his wife and children. End of story."

Silence reigned in the still room for a beat. Sunlight streamed in through a smudged window. Outside, someone sang Christmas carols, and jingle bells rang. People laughed, but in Dad's apartment, the mood was somber and full of bitterness, eating away at my insides.

I said to my brother, "There's nothing I want here. What about you?

My brother shrugged. "Same, let's go."

Dad's girlfriend stood in the kitchen doorway "Good-bye. Nice to meet you."

Troy nodded to her. "Sorry for your loss." He said to Zane, "Let's go."

The blond brushed tears from her eyes. "Can I come with you? I'll be alone for Christmas, now that Biff is gone. It'll be lonely here without him."

Troy and I locked eyes and bit our lips. We knew from experience that a holiday was not a time to be abandoned. This stranger needed comfort and companionship.

Zane said in an authoritative voice, "I'm sorry, that won't be possible. We wish you well."

She said in a wavering voice, "If his mother sends a fruit basket, like she did last year, I liked the candied apricots dipped in chocolate."

I nodded, because I liked those too, back when Grandma used to send fruit gift baskets at Christmas time. But she hadn't done that for a long time.

Zane gestured for Troy and I to go out. He said to Dad's girlfriend, "I doubt that'll happen. She's grieving for the loss of her son and very upset. Take care of yourself."

I hustled out of the apartment, ready to leave behind remnants of Dad's messy life. Zane quietly closed the door. I strode down the dim hallway, thumped down steps and hurried down a drive under redwood trees to the car.

Crossing my arms, I swayed from side to side, waited for Troy and Zane and brushed off a creeping sensation of grief that was climbing up the skin of my arms.

I shivered in the sun and stomped my feet. My brother said, "Did it creep you out, being in that apartment?"

"Yeah."

"Me too, let's get away from here."

We hopped in, and Troy started the car. In the front passenger seat, Zane turned to my brother, "Did you buy food for Christmas dinner, as your grandmother requested?"

Troy shrugged. "Not yet, we haven't had time, with everything else going on."

Zane nodded. "Let's stop at the market and pick up my order before going to the estate. That will be enough for us, so you don't need to buy more. Your grandmother is a nice person, you know. You should give her a chance to get to know her better."

I pursed my lips in the back seat and looked out the window at lamps posts decorated with white lights. My heart had been hurt once before. I wasn't about to open up and be wounded again by a family member who'd proven unworthy of trust in the past by not reaching out to us. But I'll do my best to pretend. My future depends on my brother and I pulling off a riveting, compelling Christmas family miracle. We'll drip with sincerity, create a believable loving reunion, trick our grandmother and get written into her new will. We'll fly home and be set for the rest of our lives, just like Dad promised us.

I plastered a smile on my face. "Yes, I'm looking forward to getting to know her better. She seems really nice."

My brother flicked a concerned gaze at me in the rear-view mirror, perhaps relaying I was laying it on too thick, so I said, "Thank you for taking care of her all this time. We really appreciate what you've done."

Zane stared out the window and wiped a tear from his cheek.

I nodded to myself. The gardener guy was a way into Grandma's good graces. We'll manipulate him, and he'll never suspect what we're doing behind his back.

21

FRANCESCA

Troy parked outside a quaint shop with Christmas decorations in the window and a white awning. I said, "I'll call Mom and stay here. But buy some sparkling cider and wine and a bouquet for Grandma."

Troy and Zane went inside, and I blew out a breath, sagged back in the seat and closed my eyes, spent from peering into our father's hidden life. I called Mom, and she picked up right away.

"Merry Christmas, Mom."

"Merry Christmas. How're you holding up?"

"We just went to Dad's place. It was a mess, and there wasn't anything we wanted. Troy is in the store now with the gardener."

"How are you feeling? I've been worried. I wish I could've gone with you to help."

My throat tightened with tears. "We're doing fine. We're going to Grandma's for Christmas dinner."

"Well done. You're working fast, to get an invitation like that. Remember, be nice to the gardener, because he has your grandmother's ear. Don't turn him against you."

"Don't worry, I won't. Zane's done everything for Grandma, so I can almost understand why she said she'd leave him everything. We'd never seen where Dad lived, not that I wanted to. But the whole thing is weird, being here. It seems like everyone in town drives a new car, and they live in fancy houses. It's not like Barnacle Island. I wish I was there instead."

"Nonsense. Buck up and get your job done. Make sure she leaves you her money and her home. She depends on the greedy, conniving landscaper, who has won her over, and he's grasping for everything she has. But you and your brother deserve it, because your father abandoned you. Go after what's yours and claim it."

"I will, Mom. Don't worry, I'll get it done. I need that money."

Knuckles rapped on the car window, and I flinched, looking out at the blond from Dad's apartment. I said, "I've got to go. Merry Christmas. Love you."

"Merry Christmas, hon."

I hung up and opened the car door, climbing out into cool air. The little town was decorated to the hilt, with white twinkling lights in storefronts, creating a charming scene.

Couples in T-shirts and shorts strolled past, holding hands. A woman in her early thirties wearing a jogging bra and black leggings pushed a stroller with a cooing baby. Everyone in Mill Valley was cheerful, except for me, my frosty, haughty grandmother and Troy and Zane.

I gazed at the sidewalk and let out a sigh. Death threw a shroud over our holiday. My brother and I had slammed into a cold, hard iceberg of facts. We didn't have a secret legacy in California, and our dead dad was a liar.

I turned to Dad's girlfriend. "Hi."

"I didn't get a chance to introduce myself. My name is Marcie."

I tilted my head. Dad and I rarely spoke, maybe once a year, but he never mentioned Marcie. He kept conversations superficial and cut off calls after three minutes. "How long were you together?"

She looked up at the blue sky. "Maybe three years? We didn't exactly keep track. It was a casual thing, until recently, when he asked me to move in with him."

"What did you like about him, if I can ask?"

"He was funny and kind. He was that kind of guy. I didn't expect him to die so soon."

I frowned, wishing I'd called him last week, like I meant to, but I'd put it off. Now it was too late. "It came as a surprise to us too."

"He talked about you and your brother and said good things about you."

I blinked. "He did?"

She nodded. "All the time. He bragged about you both."

I sighed. "I had no idea he ever thought about us. Thanks for telling me."

My brother and the groundskeeper emerged from the store carrying packages, and I said to Marcie, "See you later."

She wiggled her fingers in a goodbye. "Bye."

We shoved the packages in the trunk and hopped in, driving away, leaving Marcie alone on a holiday. It didn't feel right to exclude her, but this wasn't my party. I was barely on speaking terms with my grandmother, and I wasn't going to upset our plans by inviting a stranger to dinner, not when my brother and I had business to attend to. We had to think of ourselves and our futures first. For all I knew, Marcie was after a slice of the estate too.

22

ALICIA

I woke from a nap and called for Zane, but he didn't answer. I chuckled, recalling I'd told him to take the grandkids to their father's apartment. They wouldn't find any keepsakes or treasures in that heap of smelly trash. Just being there yesterday afternoon made my stomach turn. When the medics pronounced my son dead and the funeral home workers carted him away, I was glad to flee the dreary premises that reminded me of how low my son had sunk, leaving garbage and dirty dishes everywhere.

Now, I heard voices downstairs and the front door close. I smiled to myself and plotted a plan to cull out those who intended to deceive me. Picking up the phone, I dialed my attorney friend. "Merry Christmas, Parker."

Parker said in a deep voice, "Merry Christmas to you."

"I'm going to change my will, and I'd like to see you at your earliest opportunity.

"We can meet in the next few days to settle the details. What do you have in mind?"

"Well, my son passed away yesterday."

"I'm very sorry to hear that."

"It's been a shock, to have him pass first. A child shouldn't die before their mother does. It's not the natural way of things."

"And yet, sadly, it does happen all too often. But we carry on."

Someone picked up the phone elsewhere in the house. I gripped the phone tight and wondered if Zane was spying on me. Or it might be the two grandchildren who only appeared to beg for money.

Parker said, "You were saying about making changes to your will?"

I lied to see how whoever was listening would react. "I'm considering leaving everything to my two grandchildren who are visiting from Washington State. I'd like to discuss it with you."

A person on the phone line clicked off, but I also heard someone catch their breath. Perhaps two people were listening behind my back.

Parker said, "I'll have my assistant call you soon to set up a meeting. Merry Christmas."

"Merry Christmas."

I hung up, and Zane waltzed into the room. "Ready to

get out of bed? Your grandchildren are downstairs waiting for you. While you visit with them, I'll prepare dinner."

He helped me sit up in bed and waited until I got my bearings. With his help, I stood and shuffled with the walker toward the bathroom. Zane didn't appear different, but there was a subtle change in his tone this holiday afternoon, a hardness to his grip and a coldness in his voice. He might have heard the phone call with my lawyer. Or one of the visitors did. Or both.

I wobbled my way into the bathroom and shut the door in his face. I was determined to find out who was meddling with my life. I'd be sure to squash any greedy, grasping outstretched demanding hands of those who wanted my money. Whoever wanted anything from me, on Christmas of all days, and right after my son died, would come to regret it. I'd cut them out of my new will as fast as you could say jack rabbit.

23

ZANE

I stiffened my spine, pressed my lips together and served glasses of ice water to the two intruders who came to take what was promised to me. My parents told me I would inherit the estate and the old lady's bank accounts as a reward for taking care of her, acting as her servant and health care aid, in her later years.

I wrinkled my nose, recalling washing her wrinkled, withering, stinking body. I wanted a life of my own, but I did my parents' bidding, even though they're dead. "One day," they told me, "all her wealth will come to you. You'll live in the big, beautiful mansion, and their family's wrongs will be made right."

Troy held my gaze, took the crystal glass and said, "Thanks. Why don't I help you in the kitchen, and we'll get dinner ready together?"

I sniffed at the law school graduate who surely looked

down on me, someone without a college degree. Troy's father and grandmother droned on about Troy's degrees, and those conversations grated on my ears. No one paid for me to attend college. I paid my way for auto mechanic training, fueling my dream of opening a repair shop. But that died and was shoved aside when I took the job of serving her lady of elegance and entitlement. She promised me yesterday, while we waited in her son's stuffy apartment for undertakers to take away his body, that she'd make a new will and leave everything to me. But now, from what I heard when I picked up the phone, she has other plans, and her children are my adversaries.

"No thank you," I said to Troy, adding a slight bow, "I'll manage just fine."

24

FRANCESCA

Zane padded out of the library, his footsteps muffled by a thick red wool rug, and I set down a glass of ice water. I leaned in and whispered to my brother, "I heard Grandma talking on the phone when we came in, and I picked up the phone to listen."

He frowned. "You shouldn't have done that. We need her to trust us."

I inched closer, my heart thudding. "But get this, she told someone, maybe her lawyer, she was thinking about leaving everything to us."

Troy ran a hand through his hair. "It's not right to ace out the gardener. He's sacrificed his life for her for years, helping her."

I tilted my head. "It should be ours. We deserve it. Why are you having a change of heart?"

He shrugged. "He's a nice guy, and he's been doing

what we weren't. I mean, do you want to move into this humongous place, maintain it and help her day and night, being at her beck and call?"

With a sigh, I said, "No, I don't. I want to live my own life. I guess I'm selfish that way."

Troy nodded. "Me too, so let's show him some appreciation for what he's doing. I watched him at the market. He knows everyone there, because he's a frequent customer for Grandma. He doesn't deserve to be shafted, just because Dad told us something that didn't turn out to be true."

I grasped the arms of the wooden chair, gripping hard, and the whites of my knuckles showed. "But Dad said the buildings would be ours."

My brother opened his hands. "It was a fairytale, and it's gone. Let's just get to know our grandmother. Maybe Dad was wrong about her too, and she's not a snobby icicle. Maybe she has a heart underneath all her bluster."

I pouted. "I wish I could've said a last goodbye to Dad. There's so much I would've said, just to get it off my chest. It's not fair."

Grandmother thumped into the room, leaning on a walker. "That's right, dears, nothing in life is fair. And I heard you just now. I was listening right outside the door."

My bowels clenched. My brother's face turned pale. I swallowed hard, wondering if it was remotely possible to resurrect the situation and walk away with boatloads of money. If I did, I'd buy an old waterfront house on

Barnacle Island. The place had been for sale for a long time, and I'd kept my eye on it. No one wanted it because it was packed to the gills with a hoarder's stash of trash. But I could handle a mess like that, if it meant living by a beach and looking out to a brand-new horizon.

25

ALICIA

I shuffled over to an armchair and sat down, puffing out a breath. It's a good thing Zane came upstairs to help me off the toilet, because otherwise, I'd have been stuck. My flimsy arms don't have much strength anymore.

I leaned in and said to my two pesky grandchildren, "I know what you're up to, and you can forget about trying to pry money out of me. Your dad was a bum, and it's not my fault he made promises he couldn't keep."

Troy blinked. "I understand, but we just want to get to know you and share the holiday with you. It's sad Dad passed away, and it's nice to be around family who knew him."

Francesca studied the pattern in the rug, and I said in a harsh voice, "Drop the façade Francesca. I know you were counting on inheriting money when your father died, but that's not going to happen. Give up your hopes. What I told my attorney friend on the phone was for his ears alone, and I lied when I said I might leave it to you two. It was a test for whoever was listening, which turned out to be you."

My granddaughter squirmed in her seat.

I nodded. "That's right, you should be uncomfortable. I haven't heard from you in years, and that hurt my feelings. Now let's put it in the past and eat Christmas dinner. I'm hungry. How about you?"

I put my hands on my walker and tried to stand, but didn't have the strength. Troy jumped up and hurried to my side, helping me stand. I leaned on my walker and shuffled out of the room.

He motioned to his sister to join us.

In a gravelly voice, I said, "Keep up with me, young man. I don't have all day."

He stayed by my side, as I made my way to the dining room, where French doors opened to the garden. Birds chirped. Dappled sunlight made the grounds appear pleasing and pleasant.

I stopped and wiped a tear from my eye, because this was not a joyous holiday. My son was dead, and although he hadn't lived up to my expectations, I loved him all the same. No gift would bring back Biff. He was gone forever. Bereft and grieving, bitter tears were my solace on Christmas.

26

FRANCESCA

My face heated, listening to my grandmother berate me for listening in on her phone conversation. I nodded, because she was right. I shouldn't have eavesdropped, especially not when we were getting to know each other again. But I was desperate to claw back some of the money that was snatched from my hands with Dad's untimely, early death. With my future at stake, the guard rails are off, and I won't behave myself. Death is a possibility, for the gardener, for the old woman, or both of them, if we must.

I studied the pattern in the red wool carpet and shook my head. What an idiot Dad was not to make a will. And what a fool I was to believe what he'd told me and take it at face value. The abandoned little girl inside me wanted to throw a fit and weep. But it was time for me to move on and let go of the past. The failures of my father have haunted me, but I'm like him, afraid to be close to people or commit long-term. When I criticize him, I stare in the mirror and hate myself.

Troy helped our grandmother get up from a chair and they left the room. She chattered on, but her words flew past me. I dawdled behind, wondering what it would be like to live in this opulent house. There were so many rooms, I couldn't imagine it would feel cozy, like I preferred. The home my grandparents built was meant for a mess of children running through the wide halls and into the huge manicured yard. Sadly, they only had one child, my father.

Troy motioned for me to join them and go in the dining room. I stopped in my tracks and covertly watched my hardened grandmother shed tears, most likely for her departed son.

I hung my head, clasped my hands together and wished Dad well, where ever he was in the universe of deadness and after death. He wasn't the worst father, but he wasn't the best. He was a low-weight dad, a weakling on the emotional front, but he wasn't mean or volatile. He was just absent.

Grandmother pointed to a chair. "Francesca, sit there. Troy, you'll sit in your grandfather's seat at the head of the table, but help me into my seat first."

I went up to grandmother and helped her sit down. "Where will Zane sit?"

She said, "Zane won't join us tonight. It'll be just family for our Christmas dinner."

My brother and I cocked our heads and stared at each other. I resented the gardener's presence and how close he was to her, but he didn't deserve being sent to the kitchen to eat by himself on a holiday. It wasn't right.

I glanced at a large dictionary on a wooden pedestal table by a window and swallowed. "Could we please invite him too? I'd hate to ignore him after all he's done for you."

She shrugged. "Fine." She stamped her right foot on a section of carpet under the table, and a buzzer went off in the back of the house. A few seconds passed, and she sniffed. "Francesca, go check on Zane in the kitchen. See what he's doing and tell him he's invited to the dinner he's preparing for us. We'll eat with the help."

Cringing at how snobby my wealthy grandmother sounded, I shot my brother a quick look and strode away, searching for the kitchen.

27

FRANSESCA

Lights blazed throughout the house, and I made my way through a butler's pantry with glass-fronted cabinets filled with various kinds of drinking glasses. Pushing open saloon doors, I entered a large kitchen. A fan over the stove whirred, creating white noise.

Zane was bent over a task at a work table with his back to me. A pot of mashed potatoes bubbled on the stove. Slices of turkey breast in gravy sizzled in a frying pan. Scoops of red cranberry relish garnished with grated orange rind sat in a cut crystal bowl with a silver serving spoon.

Heady aromas made my mouth water. Zane bent over a white piece of paper. Curious to know what he was doing, I tiptoed over and peered over his shoulder. My mouth fell open when I read the words, Last Will and Testament.

Clutching a pen, he signed Alicia's name with a flourish.

In a loud voice, I said, "What're you doing?"

He flinched and turned, his eyes growing wide. He quickly folded the document and stuffed it in his dark blue blazer pocket. His left eye twitched. "It's nothing, nothing at all."

I stared at his eye. He was definitely planning something. My mind skittered around to the many possibilities. Not giving away one iota of what my brother and I had in mind, if it came down to a final fight with the old battle axe, I said, "I hope you won't hurt Grandma and hasten her end. She's just an innocent old woman. Besides, she said she was leaving everything to you, so why do you need a fake will?"

He shrugged and tugged on an earlobe. "If you mention this to her, I'll say you made it all up. Stay here and take care of the food. I'll be right back."

He ran out another door and pounded up a set of stairs, leaving me alone in the kitchen. Smoke billowed out from the oven. A shrieking alarm pierced the air with a high-pitched, loud noise.

Hurrying over, I turned off the oven, put on two red oven mitts and opened the oven. I fanned the air and pulled out a pumpkin pie with a burned blackened crust.

I moved to set it on the kitchen tile countertop, but a harsh voice startled me.

The pie flew out of my hands and dropped to the floor with a crack. Pumpkin filling and crust flew through the air, landing on and oozing down cupboard doors. Pieces of a glass pie dish were scattered on the linoleum floor. The kitchen smelled of smoke and ruined dinner plans, and it was my fault for distracting Zane. But it was also his fault for forging a will he didn't need, when he should've had his mind on cooking.

Grandmother's dark eyes narrowed. "What's the meaning of this? Where's Zane? He's supposed to prepare our food. I didn't authorize you to assist him or ruin a perfectly good pie, just to check on him."

I held up my hands and thought fast, deciding to not tell her Zane was up to nefarious deeds. Grandmother didn't need to know about a fake will, not yet. I'd talk it over with Troy first. My father's death was bringing out the worst and driving us to desperate acts, plotting and planning behind Grandma's back.

I gazed at the mess in the kitchen and slapped my hands against my thighs. "I told Zane he could take a break, and I'd get it ready. It's my fault. I'm sorry."

When Grandmother scowled, wrinkles in her upper lip stood out like craggy canyon walls. "Turn off that fan. You can't hear my buzzer with all the noise. I'll be in the library having a glass of sherry. You and your brother, and Zane, when he shows up, can clean up the kitchen. I expect it to be as it was before in half an hour. Tick, tock, get to work."

She shuffled away, muttering to herself.

I reached up and switched off the fan.

Troy waved his hands in the air. "Look what you did. How could you do this?"

I put my hands on my hips. "You sound just like her."

"We need to get in her good graces. Now all our efforts are undone."

I hurried over to him and whispered. "Forget about the mess for a minute. I need to tell you something."

He shook his head. "Let's not talk. We need to clean this up. Time's ticking."

I whispered to my brother, but he strode to the sink, grabbed a sponge and a bowl and a roll of paper towels.

Zane came in the kitchen, and his jaw dropped. He surveyed the disaster scene, where my culinary explosion splattered orange pumpkin everywhere. A bit of pie dangled from the white ceiling.

Zane said with a snarl, "I was only gone a minute. What happened?"

Troy ignore him and turned to me, "What did you say?"

"I'll tell you later."

"No, tell me now. I don't want any more surprises or secrets. Get it out in the open."

I pointed to the gardener, who seemed to be a nice guy, but now I knew better. He had a dark side hidden under his pleasant, bland exterior. I said, "Are you sure, with Zane here listening?"

Troy clenched his jaw. He'd become the fire-breathing dragon of a brother I feared when I was young. I specialized in sadness and burying bad feelings, but he owned anger as a way to vent.

Zane bent over a broken pie dish and, using a sponge and paper towels, he scooped up shattered bits and dumped them in the trash. As silence ticked on, he stood and stared at me, clenching his hands. "Go ahead and do what you came here for. Ruin me, so you can run away with the money. That's all you've cared about since you arrived."

Troy said, "We have a lot to do. Go ahead and say it."

I said, "Zane forged Grandma's signature on a fake will, and I saw him do it."

Troy blinked, and his eyes opened wide. He rubbed his chin.

Zane left the room.

I sighed and took a wet sponge, wiping down cupboards. We were stuck in a fragile bubble of hope that was about to burst. Disaster was about to rain down.

28

___

ALICIA

I leaned on my walker and thumped my way to the library. I ignored the petite sherry glass I usually used and took a tumbler, pouring myself two inches of the golden liquid. My knees trembled. I held on to the walker with one hand and raised the glass to my lips with the other. Taking a sip, sherry burned as it traveled down my throat, and I winced. I preferred my quiet, peaceful life, the one I had before my two grandchildren from Washington State swarmed in like locusts, consuming everything in their path.

I hesitated to sit down, knowing I'd need help to get up. Zane was preoccupied lately, It started yesterday when we found my son dead. He hadn't responded to my calls or texts, so we went over to see if anything was the matter. He always shared Christmas Eve and Christmas dinner with me, and the meals were prepared and served by Zane.

My knees felt like they might give out, so I slumped into an armchair near the tumbler and sherry decanter. Amber liquid glimmered in light coming through leaded-glass windows that my husband and I brought over from Europe.

The Christmas tree I'd instructed Zane to put up last week stood tall in a corner, decorated with red ornaments and twinkling white lights to give cheer. I blotted tears from my eyes with a tissue, because there was no joy in this house or in my heart. My son was gone.

Taking a swig of sherry, I pondered my predicament. Of the three young people under my roof, I could only trust Zane. But something fluttered behind his quick glances lately, a furtive, perhaps vindictive barbed sentiment that left me afraid. I'd hoped it would blow over when I broke the news last night I was making a new will and leaving everything to Zane. Despite that, I still sensed hidden friction between us, and I don't know the source of it.

A flutter of guilt flitted through my chest. I could've been kinder to Zane's parents, who worked as my land-scaper, driver, maid and cook. Perhaps I worked them too hard and sent them to their early graves.

I cringed and hoped that wasn't the case. I'd provided a place for the family to live. Surely that was enough reward for them.

An urgent need swept over me to go to the bathroom. I called out. "Help."

But no one came. Where was Zane? What were those three cooking up in the kitchen besides Christmas dinner?

I pulled on the arms of the chair and rocked in place, rising and standing on shaking legs. Gripping my walker, I fumed and fed an inner fire of ancient fury. I marched out of the library to the nearest bathroom, clenching my lady parts and taking shuffling steps.

With a scowl, I shut the bathroom door and sat down. Those three kids deserved a tongue lashing for ignoring me and the disaster on the kitchen floor. I'll write a new will and leave my money to charity. They should be fawning all over me, not colluding in the kitchen.

29

ZANE

I gently placed the phone on the cradle and tiptoed out of the library, stunned by what I'd just heard. Alicia planned to write a new will and leave everything to her visiting grandkids. But she hadn't seen them in years.

I nodded to myself and came up with a plan. I'd write a new will for her and forge her signature, which I've practiced. My parents coached me through what to do if it came down to the two grandchildren getting her money or me. On his deathbed, Dad murmured to me, "Make sure the money goes to you. Do what you must. You can't allow the son to have it, or the missing grandkids she never sees. Take what's yours and claim it."

I took the printed will to the kitchen and turned down the burners on the old gas stove to simmer. I needed to add Alicia's signature and store the will in a safe place. I mulled over the options of her death by drowning in a bathtub or in the swimming pool. I'd wave the will around after her death. Alicia has lived long enough.

Thinking about my parents, I wiped tears from my eyes. When I was young, my parents came home late each night and collapsed in bed, falling fast asleep, only to rise before dawn the next day to serve Alicia's endless needs. Mom taught me to plaster on a smile, ignoring resentments stewing inside.

A fan over the stove whirred. A timer for the oven dinged, but I ignored it. I've had enough, and I can't take it anymore. Alicia's son's death and the appearance of her two greedy grandchildren brought an end to my passive, pathetic state. The old lady must go.

I smiled. I'll be master of this house. I'll raise a family under this roof. My children will run through the halls, laughing.

Sucking in a breath, I pulled out a pen, scribbled the date and forged Alicia's signature with a flourish.

A voice behind me made me jump. Francesca said, "What're you doing? I hope you won't hurt Grandma."

My heart thudded, and I gathered my papers. "I'll be right back. Take care of the food. You're in charge for now."

I hurried out of the kitchen, pulse racing, and ran up the stairs to the tiny servant's room. I pulled up the thin musty old twin mattress and hid the new will under it. There was enough space for a twin bed and a night stand,

and that was it. The window was up high and too small to use in the event of a fire. I grit my teeth. Alicia and her husband designed and built this home. They knowingly put servants in a room that wasn't safe, if there was a fire.

Blowing out a breath, I wiped my hands on my pants and closed and locked the bedroom door. I had slipped out to Goodwin's hardware store off 101 to buy a lock for the door yesterday afternoon. Christmas music played in the store, and the cashier was all smiles, but I wanted to get back to the estate before Alicia discovered I was gone. Installing the lock was no problem, given what Dad taught me, but my armpits dripped with sweat. I knew I was violating the household policy of no locks on servants' quarters, but I had to keep those two grandchildren out. They wanted to take everything from me, I could feel it, like a threatening dark storm cloud hovering on the horizon.

I thumped down the back stairs to the kitchen and called on my skills of treachery, trickery and deceit. I had to keep Francesca from telling her brother and Alicia what I did with the forged will. We were pitted against each other in a battle for survival, and I had to win for my parents' sake. I wished the two money-grabbers from the north would fly home, so I could work my magic with Alicia in secret. What a surprise it'd be, for me to find her dead in a bathtub.

Pushing the swinging door open, I strode in the kitchen, and my jaw dropped. Pumpkin pie splattered the stove, the floor and the cupboard doors. Pie plate pieces were scattered on the white and black checked tiles that I mopped every day, like my mother did.

I yelled at Francesca, "What did you do? I only left for a minute."

30

TROY

I cocked my head and stared at my sister. "You've got to be making this up. The gardener wouldn't hurt our grandmother or forge a will."

But I turned to Zane and studied his clenched jaw. From the fire in his eyes and his fisted hands, he looked capable of murder. I shuddered and snapped out of my daze.

I hissed, "You can't be serious. She's just a little old lady."

Zane took a step toward me, and I inched away. He was at least two inches taller and twenty pounds of muscle heavier than me.

Francesca stepped between us. "I caught him with a fake will, and he forged Grandma's signature. He hid it somewhere in the house."

The gardener glowered and crossed his muscled arms.

I winced. His silence was a deadly weapon, and I didn't want to tick off the gardener. Scratching my chin, I said, "I'm confused. I thought you were loyal to her, but it doesn't look like that now."

Zane said, "It's none of your business how I feel or what I do. Stay out of it and run home to your little island up north. You never bothered to visit or call, so why are you here now? You just want her money, and I'm fed up with this family's entitled attitude. I'm the only who works hard. I maintain the house, the grounds, take care of your grandmother and manage her apartment buildings, with little thanks from anyone. I'm taking back control of my life, and it's high time I did. Don't get in my way. If you do, you'll regret it."

My eyebrows shot up. "I won't let you hurt Grandma. The reason we didn't see her is our father's fault."

Zane glared. "Take responsibility for your actions. My parents brought me up better than you were raised, it seems. I'm accountable. You two march in from the airport with huge expectations, kissing up to your poor ailing grandmother. Step up like adults and admit you were cruel to her."

Francesca flaps her hands at her sides. "But we only had one parent growing up. You had two."

Zane looked at my sister and I like we were dead bugs on a windshield and nothing more.

Letting out a breath, I ran through various ways to deal with the unexpected situation. When we planned our trip here with Mom, we didn't take into account the gardener's fierce feelings and motivations of his own. I'd pictured him as a mere stooge in the background, taking orders with no thoughts or desires of his own, happily helping Grandma. We came here to get the money we were owed, whether by pretense of growing close to our grandmother, by coercion and guilt, or by death.

The gardener before me was a granite rock. He staring with cold dark eyes, and it was clear he was against us. I doubted Grandma, who was no dunce, would be manipulated into giving us money. We needed to fake a will of our own and gently guide Grandma to an early death, preferably in the swimming pool in the huge back yard. No one would see us push her in. Tall hedges and a fence around the perimeter blocked out nosy prying eyes.

I sighed and wished my sister's and my solution didn't boil down to killing our grandmother. But she'd lived a long life, and it was a matter of survival. We had to correct the grave error Dad left.

Gravy in a frying pan bubbled over on the stove, hitting an open gas flame and sizzling, giving off a burning smell.

I opened my mouth to suggest we might work together, but Francesca gasped and pointed at Zane. "You have my dad's cleft chin and his thick railroad eyebrows. I didn't see it before, but now I do."

I titled my head and stared. "You're right, and there's a

strong resemblance, but it doesn't mean anything. I'm sure it's a complete coincidence."

Zane looked down, studying his scuffed white sneakers. When he met my gaze, a chill ran up my spine, and I shivered in the warm kitchen. His brown eyes were flat and filled with malice. In a low voice, he said, "I'm your brother."

31

FRANCESCA

I shrieked and clapped a hand over my mouth, fearing Grandma might hobble in and hear us. I flashed a panicked look at Troy and stared at the gardener. I didn't want another brother. I already had one. I didn't want anyone to horn in and make off with part or all of our rightful inheritance.

In a choked voice, I said, "Are you saying what I think you're saying?"

Zane nodded. "Your father pushed himself on my mother one day, when they were alone on the estate. She fought but it was no use. He overpowered her."

My stomach churned. My despicable dad sexually assaulted an employee on the property. It was almost beyond belief, but it was true. I could tell from Zane's face and his body language. "I'm so sorry. How absolutely wrong and disgusting. And your poor mother. What did she do?"

"She talked to my father, and they were afraid. Your dad threatened her, and so did our grandparents. Mom decided not to do anything. Your grandfather said they'd lose their jobs and he'd blackball them if she spoke up and told anyone. He said they'd never get work again, no matter where they moved."

I winced. "How awful. What a horrible thing to have happen. I'm sorry."

Troy cleared his throat. "I feel awful too. Dad was a horrible man. But when your mother gave birth to you, you and your family continued to live on the estate, where the assault happened?"

Zane chewed on a fingernail. "Yes, it was difficult, and it still is. When I inherit the estate, I'll tear down the pool house, where the assault happened and replace it with a rose garden, in memory of my parents."

I sighed. "I can't imagine how rough that was for your folks. Did our grandmother dote on you and treat you as her own grandchild, as she should've?"

Zane shook his head, wiping tears from his eyes. "Not one bit of affection came my way from your grandparents. When their friends came to dinner, they demanded I be left in the cottage. They were ashamed of me and hid me, because I looked like your dad when he was little."

Cocking my head, I said, "But what about in town?

Did anyone notice that you looked like a member of the family your parents served?"

Zane said, "Nope. I went to local schools, including Mt. Tam High, and no one noticed. I guess it never crossed their minds that the son of a maid and gardener might be a bastard and heir to the estate where his parents worked."

My pulse picked up. "But this is our estate, my brother's and mine, when she dies. It's not yours. I heard her on the phone earlier."

Zane looked me in the eyes. "You misunderstood. I listened in from another room, like you did, and she told me it was a ruse. She knew we were eavesdropping, and she lied. She wanted to test you."

I pursed my lips. "I doubt it was a lie. Grandma sounded sincere."

My new brother let out a bitter laugh. "You've been hidden on that island with your head stuck in the sand. You don't know the rich, like I do. They lie straight to your face without shame to get what they want."

Troy said, "Why would she lie about giving us everything in her will?"

Zane's eyes lit up. "Because she's fooling you. There's already a signed will giving me everything, like she said when she called you Christmas Eve. It's all set in stone. She asked me to print out a fake will and make sure Francesca saw me forging her signature."

I opened my hands. "That's why she sent me into the

kitchen just now. But why did we bother to come down here, if it was already set up? What's going on?"

Zane said, "What's going on is you've confirmed her worst fears. You're only after her money. Just like your father, all you care about is gliding along on her dollar."

Troy glanced toward the dining room. "Wait, where's Grandma? We need to see how she's doing. She might need our help."

The three of us sprang into action, working as one unit. We turned off burners on the stove, left the sticky mess on the floor and trotted down halls, calling for her. If we'd been young children, it would've been a game, but it wasn't.

Acid rose from my gut, and I swallowed bile. My dad was a horrible man, far worse than I'd imagined, and his parents covered up for him. I made a face and didn't want anything more to do with this side of the family. Grandma's dirty money was tainted with filthy secrets, and Zane deserved it far more than we did. My brother and I were abandoned, but Zane's truth about his birth father was erased by our wealthy grandparents. They covered up a crime.

My stomach lurched, and I threw open a door, barging into a bathroom. My grandmother was sitting on the toilet, hunched over. I retched into the sink and coughed up dreadful hate for my dead disgusting dad.

I wiped my mouth on a hand towel and yelled out the door, "I found her. We're in a bathroom by the library."

32

ALICIA

Sitting on the toilet, tears streamed down my cheeks. Over the years, I had to bury the truth about my son being Zane's true father. I was tired of telling lies.

My heart fluttered, and my chest grew tight. My jaw ached.

I ran a hand over my lower back, which hurt. Would it be so bad to die now and let go? Yes, it would.

I grimaced. I'd be humiliated when people found me on the toilet. What an embarrassing final note to a carefully curated life that'd be. I couldn't let it happen.

"Help," I called in a weak voice. But with the bathroom door closed, no one heard me. I'd left my medical alert button by the bedside, as I often did, thinking I was immortal, and I'd never need to use it.

I reached out a feeble, trembling hand, but the

intercom on the wall was too far away. Alone on the toilet, I slumped over and put a hand to my chest.

This wasn't the glorious end I wanted for my elegant life. I didn't want to die on a toilet.

"Help."

With my last breath, I wheezed, "I'm sorry, Zane. I'm sorry. I should've treated you better."

33

FRANCESCA

My brothers ran in the bathroom and crowded around Grandmother. I said, "I think she's dead."

Zane reached out and felt for a pulse. "She's definitely dead. We need to clean her up and get her in bed. She wouldn't want strangers to see her this way. What an undignified end that would be. She'd be humiliated."

Troy touched Zane's arm. "Stop. Don't move her. If we do, we could be accused of killing her. Leave her be and call 911. Did she have a DNR?"

Zane nodded. "She does. She didn't want to be revived, if something like this happened. She was ready to go."

I said, "Maybe her dying here is a fitting end, for someone who covered up the truth about what Dad did."

Zane glared. "Don't speak ill of her. I won't allow it, even after death. She was following your grandfather's orders, even after he passed away. He had a far reach from the grave."

Troy sniffed the air. "What stinks? Did she throw up in the sink over there?"

"That was me. I'll wash the sink."

Troy grabbed my wrist. "Don't. Leave everything as it is. We need to prove this was an accident, and we had no part in her death. I don't want to go to jail for something I didn't do."

I said, "I'll call 911 and stay with her body."

Zane nodded. "I'll grab the DNR from the kitchen drawer. She was too vain to post it on the refrigerator, like her doctor suggested."

Troy stood and wiped his eyes. "It's a shame we never got to know her."

Zane paused at the doorway. "She was unknowable and a cold witch, as your father said to me once. But she did the best she could, under the circumstances. She grew up dirt poor and they ate dandelion soup for dinner. She told me money mattered most to her, above all else."

Troy nodded. "I'll meet the EMTs at the door. And the police will probably do an investigation into her death. Hang on, we'll get through this together."

When my brothers left the bathroom, I pulled out my phone and called 911, reporting that we thought our grandmother was dead of natural causes.

Standing there watching her shriveled corpse lean to the side, I said, "I wish you'd told us the truth. I would've liked to know I had another brother. He seems like a nice guy, and he's defending you, I'll have you know. But you could've reached out to us when Dad left. We never heard from you. We thought you didn't love us and didn't want to hear from us."

The EMT's arrived, crowding the small room, and I stepped out to the hallway, glad to be away from the stink of death, the corpse and the stench of my vomit. My brothers and I crowded together in the hallway, and Troy's shoulders shuddered as he wept for the grandmother we'd never know.

Zane wiped tears from his eyes with the back of his hands, but I was unfazed. In fact, it was a relief to see the woman who loomed large in my father's tales as an ornery witch finally succumb to death. All my hopes for a happy reunion on Christmas day were dashed and the past made clear. I hadn't missed out on much, except for Zane's silent suffering and my dad's deep dark secret about his unacknowledged offspring.

Taking a deep, calming breath, I patted my brothers' broad shoulders. Grandma was pronounced dead. The police arrived, asked questions and took notes. An officer told us the body could be removed, and the mess around the toilet and in the sink could be cleaned up.

I called Fernwood Funeral Home, and two workers, one short and one tall, came for Grandma's body. They lifted her from her throne and placed her on the floor in the hallway, zipping her into a black body bag. They carried her out to an unmarked van waiting in the driveway.

My brothers and I held hands as she left the house for the last time. I let go of their fingers and waved as the workers closed the van doors. Zane pressed a button to open the black wrought iron gates, and the van slowly drove away.

"Goodbye," we said, speaking in soft voices full of loss, loathing and love. Lined up like children ready for inspection, we were waiting for the love we'd never received, the words of encouragement that never came and for a father to apologize to the woman he'd assaulted.

I shrugged. "I guess it's over. At least the truth came out. And I'm glad to know you're my brother."

Zane nodded. "She guarded the secret to protect her reputation. She didn't care how I felt. She never once said she loved me."

Troy went over and clapped Zane on the shoulder. "I'm sorry about what you and your family went through. But we're here for you now."

A whiff of pure greed leaked through my skin, and I sighed at how close I'd come to having plenty of money. My chance of inheriting a building was gone. The game was over before it began, and Grandmother controlled the rules. I didn't stand a chance against her.

I said, "I guess I'll go clean up the smelly mess in the bathroom."

Zane said, "I'll get dinner ready. Are you hungry?"

"I could eat," I said, surprised to find I was famished.

Troy nodded. "I'll help you in the kitchen. I'll do anything to do avoid Francesca's job in the bathroom."

I glided down the hall and scrubbed the bathroom, bringing it back to life. Flicking off the lights, I left the door open for fresh air to filter in, but we'd never completely get rid of the stink of wrongdoings in this mansion.

I hurried down the hall to join my brothers and eat Christmas dinner together. We had a surprise sibling, and the dynasty of lies ended with Grandma's death. I wished we'd known about our brother earlier. But at least now, we had a chance, in the clear California sunlight.

34

ZANE

Troy and I cleaned the kitchen floor, wiped down pumpkin pie splatter on white cabinets and threw the rest of the broken pie plate in the trash. Washing my hands and drying them on a hand towel, I moved aside for Troy to take his turn at the sink.

I took a deep breath and crossed my arms, leaning back against the white tiled countertop. Alicia was willing to spend loads of money on cars and clothes, but not in areas where outsiders never saw. The kitchen was my parents' and my domain. No guests ever set foot here.

I said, "So, how's this going to work?"

Troy flicked water off his fingers and took the towel I tossed to him. "You mean us being brothers?"

My pulse quickened, because I'd broached a topic I'd always wanted to over the years. I'd dreamed of this day, but now I doubted they'd welcome me into their tight fold. I didn't have any family left, now that our grand-mother was dead. "Sure, that's what I mean. I was an only child, and I'm not sure how to be a brother."

He grinned and drew me into a hug. "Let's take it day by day. But you're always welcome to stay with us on Barnacle Island."

Francesca came in the kitchen and screwed up her face. "That was the most disgusting clean up job I've ever had to do, but it's done. It's all fresh and sparkling clean in there now."

I nodded. "That's the first time someone else has cleaned in this house except for me and my parents, in many, many years. Thank you for doing that."

She shrugged. "It's about time someone else did it. Let's eat."

We sat around the dining table, gathered together at the far end by a large dictionary, and ate turkey with gravy and mashed potatoes. We toasted with sparkling wine.

Francesca raised her glass. "To my living without expectations of wealth arriving at any minute, miracu-lously solving my problems. Merry Christmas."

"Same here," Troy said, raising his glass.

"Absolutely," I said. "I'll drink to that. And I hope I'll never hear that buzzer hidden under the rug to ring for service again. In fact, I'll rip it out myself. Merry Christmas."

Looking at my newfound sister and brother, I realized the negative drama had been created by my biological father. He'd lied to them and created a hunger for what they couldn't have. One day, I might give them each a gift of money in memory of our icicle queen of a grandmother. If they behave themselves, that is. I'll keep my eye on them, because I know I can't trust those who are closest. Family, I've learned, can be vicious.

The phone rang, and I got up to answer it. "Hello?"

"Zane, this is Parker, your grandmother's attorney. I was notified that she passed away today, and I called to say I'm sorry to hear that."

I swallowed tears, because those you love can hurt you by showing cold indifference that skewers the heart. But I know Alicia loved me. I'm sure of it. That's why she left me the estate.

"If you're available right now, I'd like to come by and read you her will. It's a bit unusual, my coming over, but we were family friends, and I think she'd want me to let you know the contents of her will right away."

My throat closed tight, and I managed to say, "But I already know the contents of her will. She told me she left everything to me before she died."

Francesca and Troy shot me worried looks.

Parker said in a deep voice, "I'm afraid that's not the case. It's a bit more complicated than that. Are Troy and Francesca there?"

"Good. Keep them there. I'll want to speak to the three of you at the same time. I'll be over soon."

35

ZANE

The doorbell rang, and I hurried to answer it. My hands were cold. My armpits prickled with sweat. I cautiously opened the door to a man in his late sixties with gray hair. I'd met him before when my grandparents had parties, and he struck me as a kind man.

We shook hands and I welcomed him inside, taking his coat. I said, "Let's go in the dining room. My sister and brother are waiting for you in there."

When I hung up the phone and told my siblings what was about to happen, we rushed around clearing the dining table and tidying up the kitchen, putting food away. Now, the place was spotless and the dining table gleamed.

I said, "Can I get you something to drink?"

Parker looked over his glasses. "No, thank you."

We entered the dining room, where Francesca stood looking out a window to the garden and pool that I maintained.

Troy stopped pacing the rug and strode over to us, shaking Parker's hand. Parker introduced himself to my siblings, and I said, "Let's sit down."

I sat and wiped a smile from my face. I'd waited for this moment for many years, plotting and planning with my parents. I'd wanted the old lady to die and get what she deserved. For her to pass away on the toilet was the ultimate humiliation for her. How she must have hated that. She never sensed my disdain for her. I shoved my resentment down a deep well when I was with her and covered up my hatred for her and her son.

Parker took a seat and opened his leather briefcase, taking out a stack of papers. He said, "Let's begin."

I nodded and was sure I knew was he was going to say. But he spoke for a few minutes, and his words became a blur. I shook my head to clear it from a fog of confusion, not sure I'd understood.

My jaw clenched. Surely, my two siblings wouldn't get a dime of Grandmother's money. They hadn't worked for it. They hadn't called or sent cards. They'd glided along in bubbles up north, living selfish lives, while I'd slaved away, working night and day.

Parker said, "Any questions?"

I swallowed. "Did you say Grandmother intended us

to share this house? And divide up the apartment buildings, so we each get one?"

Parker nodded. "That's right."

"But she gave me no indication this would happen. Are you sure you're right? And my siblings live far away, so how would this work? She told me specifically I'd inherit the house and all of her estate."

Parker adjusted his glasses. "Your grandmother wanted you three to come to an agreement and work it out. Do you think you can do that?"

I thrust my hands under the table and clenched them. Disappointment bubbled up inside, because this wasn't right. What I was promised was ripped from my hands. She lied to me. Everything I'd counted on was gone.

Francesca gnawed on a fingernail, seemingly dazed by the news.

I nodded. Grandmother's true will sent a rogue wave crashing over me, taking me out to sea on a riptide. The bitter old woman must be having a last laugh from the grave. Everything I thought I knew was wrong.

I ground my teeth and plotted secret revenge on my two siblings. I'd never show them how I truly felt, but justice must be served in the end. Someone had to hurt, and it wouldn't be me.

Troy leaned in, drumming his fingers on the table. "The problem for me is it doesn't seem fair to Zane. He's the one who did all the work for many years. He suffered from our father's actions, as did his poor mother and the man who brought him up as his son. I understand Grandma wanted us to get to know each other and share, but I think the house and the property and the car, at the very least, should go entirely to Zane. Do you agree, Franny?"

She nodded. "Yes, I do. Zane's done all the heavy lifting, while we did nothing. We took it for granted that we'd each inherit a building. I'm ashamed of how we acted, now that I'm here and hearing the truth of what happened. We shouldn't share this house. Zane, you deserve it. It should be all yours."

Parker said, "Zane, what do you think of their suggestion?"

I pressed my lips together in a thin line and thought about my dear departed parents who served the monsters who owned this mansion. "There's no way to make things right, but this will be a start. But I may find that living here is too uncomfortable for me, given my memories and how my mother was treated. I may decide to sell it one day. But I'll try living in it and see how it goes. If the ghosts of the past don't haunt me, I may raise my own children here someday. Thank you for your kind gesture. It means a lot to me, especially since we've just met."

Parker said, "About the three apartment buildings your grandmother owned. Do you want to pick who gets what, or shall I randomly assign them to you?"

Francesca wrinkled her nose. "I'd rather not own the

one where Dad died. When I was there, I felt too many reminders of the past."

I said, "That building is high maintenance, because of moisture coming from the nearby creek. I'd rather not own it, because there's where the man who forced himself on my mother lived. It's a daily reminder of the horror she went through and how this family covered up the truth with threats."

Troy scratched his stubbled chin. "I'll take that building, and I'd like to let Dad's girlfriend live in the apartment he had for the rest of her life rent-free. At least his death can mean one good thing."

I made a face and rested a hand on my churning gut. "Good riddance to him. I'm glad he's gone. It couldn't come soon enough."

Francesca gave me a quick nod, and Troy did the same. Although they've sat back for years and acted entitled, maybe they're not as bad as I'd assumed.

Parker pushed the papers back in the briefcase and stood. "I'll be in touch and see my way out. You three have a lot to talk about. Good night, and Merry Christmas."

I stood and blew out a relieved breath. "Good night."

I glanced around the dining room, where my parents worked as maid and butler, obeying their employer's orders, no matter when and why they called. The house was mine, just like my parents intended when they trained me to be my grandmother's servant and right-hand man. We'd done it, and my folks must be clapping from the grave.

36

FRANCESCA

Four months later, Troy and I were back in Mill Valley, but this time we were driving with our brother Zane to Rodeo Beach. We'd skipped holding funeral services, given our mixed feelings about Grandmother and Dad. Most of Grandma's friends died years before anyway.

Troy paid off his student loan debt. I bought a run-down house by the water on Barnacle Island, and we paid Zane to maintain our apartment buildings and be our property manager. Zane tore down the pool house and planted a rose garden, in memory of his parents.

At the beach, I kicked off my sneakers and stepped onto warm, soft sand, squishing it between my toes. Misty sea air wafted past, and waves crashed on shore. Beach grass swayed in a steady breeze. Surfers sat on surf boards, waiting for the perfect wave to carry them forward.

I ran, my bare feet pounding on hard sand along the waterline, and caught up with my brothers, tagging them on the back. "Tag, you're it," I yelled into the wind.

Zane and Troy grinned at the challenge and ran after me, and I laughed with all my might. Everything was going to be better than fine. I was riding a wave that I hoped would never end, with my two brothers by my side.

Next up will be *The Gas Station Motel,* a thriller!

A young woman stops with her cat at a motel and wakes with her wrist strapped to a hospital bed. Members of a crime ring will operate and take her kidney, leaving her for dead. Can she outsmart them?

Hear about my new books by signing up for my author newsletter on my website www.susanspechtoram.com

Read *Shore Lodge*
A grieving widow. A greedy son. A locked psych ward. She must escape to rescue her dog and reclaim her home. "A nail-biter!"

Thank you for reading *A Chilling Christmas Eve*! Please let other readers know what to expect by posting ratings and reviews on Goodreads, Amazon and BookBub.

Follow me on BookBub for updates

My Facebook author page is Susan Specht Oram Author
If you're on YouTube, look for my author channel
@susanspechtoramauthor
featuring audiobooks, author chats and nature photography.

Thank you for reading my books!

ABOUT THE AUTHOR

Susan is writing mysteries-thrillers and creative nonfiction. Previously, she served as senior director of corporate communications for biotechnology companies. Susan worked as an activity aide in an upscale nursing home's secure psychiatric unit. She was a potter and painter with an art studio in Seattle and has also worked as a market researcher, a nurse's aide, a waitress, and a library page. Her essays have been published in Mothering Magazine, Twins Magazine and Utne Reader. Susan grew up near Detroit, Michigan. She lives in a windy part of the Pacific Northwest with her husband and rescue dog.

Mysteries-Thrillers
    Shore Lodge
    The Thieves
    Cabin Eight
    Secrets at the Café
    The Mother's Threat
    Under Jackson Bridge
    Missing Man
    By Midnight

The Winter Storm

The Cold Night

Avalanche

These Lies

A Chilling Christmas Eve

The Gas Station Motel

NONFICTION TITLES

Creative Nonfiction: Strangers on a Train Series
Green Light
The Train
Canoe
Soup Kettle
Bathtub
Phone Call
Watering Can
Waterfall
Strangers on a Train Series collection (Books 1-8)

Humorous fiction
Boating with Buddy, a report from a canine corre-
spondent

Nonfiction

Brief business books on investor relations, crisis communication and public relations